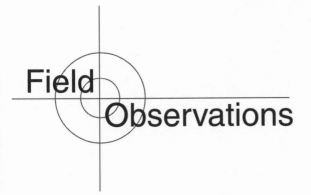

Field Observations

Field Observations

Stories by Rob Davidson

University of Missouri Press
Columbia and London

University of Missouri Press, Columbia, Missouri 65201
Printed and bound in the United States of America
5 4 3 2 1   05 04 03 02 01

Cataloging-in-Publication data available from
the Library of Congress

ISBN 0-8262-1334-0

㊾™ This paper meets the requirements of the
American National Standard for Permanence of Paper
for Printed Library Materials, Z39.48, 1984.

Design and composition: Vickie Kersey DuBois
Cover design: Kristie Lee
Printer and binder: The Maple-Vail Book Manufacturing Group
Typefaces: Frutiger, Palatino

For Sophie

Contents

Acknowledgments

Some of the stories in this collection appeared in the following periodicals: "Inventory" won a 1997 AWP Intro Journals project award for fiction and appeared in *Hayden's Ferry Review*; "The Hillside Slasher" appeared in *The Bryant Literary Review*; "A Private Life" appeared in *Another Chicago Magazine*; "Maintenance" appeared in *Apostrophe* and, in earlier form, in *The Pikestaff Forum* (published as "In Alien Country"); "What We Leave Behind" appeared in *Thin Air*.

For their help and encouragement, I would like to thank Patricia Henley, Linda Rogers, Steve Yarbrough, and the many teachers, friends, and colleagues who read and critiqued these stories over the years.

Field Observations

Inventory

I walked among the hutches as I smoked. Rabbits hopped back and forth across the sawdust and straw lining their cages, or lay piled together in a shady corner, sleeping. There were many of them, and they were quiet. I'd taken to spending my breaks this way, with the rabbits. Something about them calmed me—the slow, patient munching, the ability to sit still, curled up and comfortable-looking even on the hottest of days. They seemed content.

I heard the scrape of the steel fire door and turned to see who'd opened it. Harold bent down and wedged a pop can in the doorway, leaving a narrow gap. He walked hurriedly across the sandy clearing, his belly jiggling beneath his untucked T-shirt. His faded, tight jeans had long gray streaks over the thighs where he rubbed his hands all the time. He stopped next to me, at the edge of the hutches. His head began to bob back and forth rapidly, and then a belch exploded from his mouth.

"God damn, Harold," I said.

"What?" he said. "I have to do it somewhere." Inside the warehouse he generally kept it to a long, low *FFFFF,* but that was bad, too, especially when it wafted across the packing table at me. "Can I bum a smoke?" he asked. I held the pack out. He fumbled at the cardboard lid with his chubby fingers, taking my last cigarette. I lit it for him. Harold held a cigarette like a joint, and he inhaled it the same way: one long drag followed by a series of rapid, short puffs.

"You like these rabbits, don't you?" he asked.

"Yeah, I guess so," I said. "They're quiet."

"You ever eat 'em?"

"Rabbit? Hell no."

"I thought maybe in the Army they fed you rabbit. What do they feed you in the Army, anyway? K-rations and shit?"

"They make you dig for tubers," I said.

"What?"

"Shut up, Harold."

"You're a queer bastard," he said. He took a long drag off his cigarette, then bent down and blew smoke into a rabbit's face. The rabbit closed its eyes. Other than the perpetually twitching nose, it didn't move. Harold laughed. "Silly rabbit," he said, "Trix are for kids." Harold stood up. "You see that?"

"Harold, you're a genius."

He furrowed his brow and said, "You're a queer bastard."

The fire door opened again and Jerry's narrow, silver-haired head popped into the hot sun. The word that defined Jerry was *groomed.* Never had a hair out of place. Pressed shirt and tie every day—Italian silk. He was fond of purple. It bugged me.

"Stalker!" he yelled. Jerry yelled most of the time. It was his usual way of communicating. "Stalker!" he shouted again.

"Yeah?" asked Harold, not turning around.

"I thought I told you that one of the phonies has a flickering lightbulb."

"You did," said Harold.

"Then why did I just get another call complaining that it hasn't been fixed?"

"I had to go to the post office."

"You went to the post office at one. It's almost three now. What've you been doing all afternoon?"

"Playing with myself," he said, laughing. It was at moments like that that I wondered if Harold had any idea what the rest of the people in the warehouse thought of him.

"Well, get your hands out of your pants and get over there and change it. Now!"

"Yes, *sir*," Harold said.

"And quit propping this door open with your frigging Coke cans. You want to pay the air-conditioning bill?" He kicked the can out into the sand and the heavy door slammed shut with a ka-chunk.

"Asshole," muttered Harold. He pinched the cherry off his half-smoked cigarette and stuck the remainder in the chest pocket of his T-shirt, then walked around the corner of the building.

Harold's job title at B&G Software was Assistant Office Facilitator. To all of us in the warehouse, he was the gofer. He ran to the Eden Prairie post office or the SuperAmerica, sorted and delivered the office mail, and kept the kitchen stocked with coffee, salt and pepper, and plastic forks. He was the one you called if the microwave in the lunch room bombed. Or if a lightbulb burned out. Not a tough job. But Harold was slow and he forgot things.

Jerry had started the nickname, Stalker, and was the only one to use it to Harold's face on any kind of a regular basis. Behind Harold's back, however, the name stuck. Sure, it rhymed with his last name, Walker. But it was more than that. It was Harold's face. When most people relax, their facial features soften. They look pensive, sad, bland. Not Harold. His normal face was a heavy, fixed stare, a stare from somewhere far behind the deep-set eyes. A stare you imagined a rapist or a mugger having. It didn't help that Harold was overweight, pale, and had a large bald spot he tried to cover with wisps of oily black hair. Then there was the belching.

Harold was really different during his job interview. Quiet. Fidgety, I remember, but I'd put that down to nerves. Everyone's nervous at a job interview, if they want the job. I thought Jerry and I had hired the right guy. Early thirties. Eager. But by the end of his second or third month in the warehouse it was clear Harold was screwing up. The nickname started. People were complaining about his personal habits. So I took Harold out to lunch and tried to explain to him how Jerry and I expected things to go around the warehouse. It concerned me that he didn't seem to be catching on. I mean, Jerry and I went through the whole job search process together, but after we'd narrowed it down to three can-didates, he left the final decision to me. I'd be working with him the most.

The talk had obviously done no good.

"During Basic," I remember the drill sergeant saying the first day, "everything and everyone is the same: shit. You're all shit. You're going to carry shit, memo-rize shit, repeat shit. You're going to climb shit, dig shit, fall in shit, and pass the shit down the line. You're going to sleep in shit. You're going to do all kinds of shit. And if you fuck up, you'll eat shit."

Basic. Everyone goes through it, and everyone hates it. The key to survival is your team, and at the simplest level, that's your squad. One notch above that, your platoon. You've got to work together, or you'll all go down. Eight weeks. You have to bond. It's that simple.

Paul Horton was in my squad, and Horton just never fit in. Horton did stupid stuff, like ask the drill sergeant how many push-ups he could do, so Horton could bet-ter him. Horton thought he was showing off, showing how hard-core he was, but you don't make it through Basic by challenging your drill sergeant. There was the time our entire platoon got woken up in the middle of the night and ordered to hump the five clicks to the rifle range, double-time. On entering the range we were commanded to drop and shoot. Horton gets there and his gun isn't clean. He's got pebbles in there, or some-thing. Pebbles in his rifle! And he's slow to clean it in the field, to boot. The platoon leader's shouting at the squad leader. The squad leader's shouting at Horton.

Horton ended up making it tough on all of us.

The drill sergeant punished the entire platoon for Horton's mistakes, so the platoon punished Horton. At first, some of the guys just pushed him around, shouting at him. The platoon leader took him out behind the wood shed. Still, Horton wouldn't wake up. The fist-fights started. Horton knew he didn't fit in, but he didn't care. He took pride in being the fuckup loner. In Basic, that's bad enough. But if you make your platoon do a second midnight run to the rifle range and an extra sentry duty, you pay.

Horton got a blanket party. Some of the platoon wait-ed in his quarters, lights out, until Horton got off sentry. When he walked in they threw a wool blanket over his head, pulled him down to the floor, and laid into him. They really did him in. They let him know how they felt. I wasn't there, but I knew about it. He was in my squad. I could've warned him, and part of me says I should have. But it would've only delayed the inevitable, and I would've lost favor with the platoon. It's a crappy spot to be in, knowing something like that was coming and yet knowing you weren't going to do a thing about it. Even though I felt rotten not warning Horton, there was never any question in my mind that I'd stand back and let the platoon beat him. That's justice during Basic. That's how issues are settled in a platoon. I'm not saying it's right. But that's how it is. And the bottom line is it was Horton's fault for not figuring that out.

No one in the warehouse knew Jerry raised rabbits until after his wife left him. We all knew about the wife—at least we knew Jerry's side of it. She left him, but somehow won the house. He moved into an apartment in Richfield and suddenly had all these rabbits to deal with. When he set the hutches up in the sandy clearing out behind the warehouse, that really threw us for a loop. I mean, you just don't figure a loud little guy running around in tailored shirts and loafers for a rabbit breeder.

To understand it, you had to see him with his rabbits. Once I surprised him as he stood over a hutch. I had an order he had to sign. Usually, I came out of the fire door, which Jerry would've heard, but that day I used the side door for some reason and walked around the corner of the building. There he stood, holding his silk tie against his belly, stroking the head of a bunny whose nose twitched against the chicken wire. "Yes, little buddy," he said, and, "Oh, you need your water changed, don't you?" Something like that. When he finally heard me he tried to act like it was no big deal, but his face flushed bright red. I think he expected me to give him shit. I was struck dumb, frankly; in the ten months I'd worked with him, I'd never heard him speak like that. I hadn't thought it possible.

After that, I'd ask him questions about the rabbits once in a while. Stuff like, How long does a rabbit live? I had no idea. Jerry would explain whatever I wanted to know. How often to feed them. When to breed them. What the gestation period was. He was very proud of his rabbits. "Once a rabbit has been domesticated," Jerry told me, "it's totally dependent on you. My rabbits could never make it in the wild. They need me."

It was the only topic Jerry could discuss like a normal human being. I liked talking to him about the rabbits, but that was all I liked talking to him about. He made it pretty hellish around the warehouse—worse than any-thing I ever saw in the Army, outside of Basic. I was good at my job, so I never caught hell. Still, Jerry was enough to make me want to quit.

Two weeks out of Basic my C.O. pulled me aside and asked me where I wanted to go in "today's Army." I didn't know what he meant, but I soon learned. Unless you want to go R.A.—Regular Army—you'd better have a skill.

What did I learn in the Army? Inventory control. I worked in a munitions warehouse at Fort Bliss, in El Paso. A pretty easy job, really. No long training mis-sions in the desert, no war games. I figured I was suit-ed for it. When I was a kid, my mother found it incred-ible that no matter how cluttered and messy I kept my room, I always knew exactly where everything was. I'm still like that. I'm not a neat freak. Far from it. I'm kind of a slob. But whenever I have to get something, even something small, like the key to an old trunk or my Swiss Army knife, I know right where to find it. My mother said I had a photographic memory. At Fort Bliss, some of the guys called me anal. Neither is true. It's just that I remember.

The Army is a country-within-a-country. And, like anywhere else, it's full of contradictions. You've got superiors who bark orders and make threats, but then they let you skip off base and shag whores and buy dope and generally get away with a hell of a lot. So maybe you don't take that authority crap all that seri-ously. Maybe you laugh at it and consider it a big joke. Then you climb a couple notches and they land you on top of a munitions warehouse with a half dozen PFCs under you, these green fucks straight out of Basic, or, worse, lifers who've been in longer than you and who still don't know a damn thing, or foreigners whose only skill is the ability to take orders, and suddenly you're the one barking commands and drawing the lines . . . and looking the other way.

What I did at B&G wasn't all that different from what I did in the Army: I managed the floor of a warehouse. I was in charge of inventory control, shipping and receiving, packaging. I was just doing it for an accounting software firm. Fiscal year-end and Christmas were our big seasons; I'd been through one Christmas, and compared to the titanic loads we shipped out of Fort Bliss during Desert Storm, life at B&G was serene. The ultimate difference between B&G and the Army was that, in the Army, you surrendered yourself to authority. You had to. That was part of being in the Army. I did what I did at Fort Bliss because I was ordered to, and, with a fixed termination date in mind, it didn't bother me much. At the end of your four years you might get offered a commission, or you might re-up. Or, like me, you go civvy. I returned to Minneapolis and started looking for a job doing what I'd done in the Army, thinking it'd be all right, that I didn't mind it and I could make a decent living at it.

I lived with my older brother, Tom, for a couple of months. Tom complimented me on having bulked up in the service, and recommended I take some time off from work. "Let your mind breathe," he'd said. Tom had worked his way through law school. He had a good job at a firm downtown, but he was worn out.

"Look at me," he'd say. "I'm twenty-nine, single, and a burnout. I haven't had a vacation since I was eighteen. Don't run back to work, Scott. Trust me. You're twenty-three. Go blow some steam." But I wanted a job the instant I got out of the Army because for the first time in my life I felt like I was free to do what I wanted. I had a skill and I had experience. I wanted my own apartment. I wanted a car. I wanted a *life*.

A year later, it didn't add up. Sure, I had a two-bedroom in Burnsville and a '93 Camaro. But every day at the warehouse was the same. The same screaming fits from Jerry. The same orders coming in and going out. The same routine of sitting at the terminal and updating the inventory every morning, listening to Harold belch. The same smoke breaks out back with the rabbits who just seemed to take it all in stride, uncomplaining and content.

Oh, to be a rabbit.

I knew I could quit. I'd thought about it. But what would I do? Tom recommended temporary work. "It's a good way to try out a few different things," he said. "Think about going to school and getting a degree." Tom said a lot of things, and I finally quit asking him what to do because he always had an answer.

Tom said I was spinning my wheels, wasting time. I preferred to think of it as taking stock. I was doing inventory, checking what I had and gauging what I'd need. Inventory can't be done overnight. It's a lengthy process. But, sooner or later, it has to end. You have to admit what you have and what you don't have, and then you need to get on with it. Inventory is cyclical; you know you'll have another chance to do a recount later.

❀

I finished my cigarette and headed around the corner of the building. I didn't like going in the side door. I felt like I was watched every time I went in there. In back, in the warehouse, we wore jeans and T-shirts. You didn't need a college degree or a great résumé. But out front it was ties and pressed shirts; it was B.A., C.P.A., M.B.A., whatever. I'm talking about programming, Q.A., sales, and phone support—the "phonies." Phonies were the worst. They thought they ran the place. They knew the software, top to bottom. They had to deal with the pissed-off customer. They charged by the minute and by the program fix, if there was a bug (which there usually was at B&G). The side door led you right into phonie central, and maybe it was just me, but I felt hostility there. I mean, no one ever said anything or did anything. It was just this feeling you got that they thought they were above you, that you were just a warehouse guy.

When I walked in the side door, Harold was just climbing up a stepladder. A three-foot fluorescent light tube leaned against a cubicle wall nearby. Harold had the wrong ladder, first. It was too short, and he was too big for it. So when he got up to the top step, it started wiggling back and forth. Then he had trouble getting the old tube out. The more Harold pulled and yanked, the more the ladder wiggled. I was on my way to ask Harold if he needed a hand when he fell. I saw it all as if it were in slow-motion: the ladder toppled off to the left with Harold's feet, sending his body in a clockwise twist. The ladder fell on top of the new fluorescent tube, which exploded. Then the old tube fell out of the ceiling and exploded, too.

When I opened my eyes, I saw bits of glass at my feet.

Phonies poked their heads up above their cubicles and remarked about the noise. I ran over to Harold, who lay face down on the floor, his right forearm outstretched and on top of one end of a tube. Glass crunched under my boots. A small trickle of blood was already soaking the carpet. I asked if he was all right.

"Arrrr," he moaned—a good sign. That was his typical response when someone confronted him with a mistake. He sat up carefully. It looked like some glass was in his arm. A fine white powder surrounded the area where the tubes had broken. I wondered if it was toxic.

Jerry appeared around the corner. As a small group of phonies congregated to look at the mess, I explained what had happened. Jerry stood, imposing despite his short, thin frame, nodding at what I said. When I'd finished, he knelt down next to Harold.

"What is it with you, boy?" Harold looked up at Jerry with that heavy stare. A chair appeared from the next cube over, and two phonies lifted Harold up and into it. "He can't do anything right, can he?" Jerry asked me.

I shrugged my shoulders. "How're you feeling?" I asked Harold.

"A little . . . I don't know."

"You had enough padding to cushion the fall, didn't you?" asked Jerry.

I looked at Jerry. He smiled and raised his eyebrows.

It was decided that Harold should go to the emergency room, and that I would drive him there. Someone wrapped Harold's arm in gauze, and then he stood. The group of phonies that had clustered around the scene began to disperse. I heard one say, "And he's the one who's supposed to clean up something like this."

Two phonies helped Harold walk out to the parking lot. Jerry and I followed. We stood at the back of Harold's rusty Ford Fairmont as Harold was helped into the passenger seat.

Jerry spoke in that loud, sharp voice. Too loud, I thought. "He's gonna cost this company a pile in liability, Scott, he keeps it up. Fat Boy's not cost effective. Think about it. He's only been here six months." It was true, sort of. In six months Harold had hit his head while digging into a steel storage cabinet (resulting in a light compress), sprained a wrist trying to lift a pallet (he had to wear a wrist brace for two weeks), and nearly sliced a finger off while cutting paper (he wrapped his finger in so much gauze his pinkie looked like a carrot).

"Maybe we should talk about it later," I said.

Dennis, one of the phonies, tossed me the car keys as he headed back to the building. I wondered what Dennis thought about Harold, Jerry, and me. I wondered what Dennis was going to say once he got inside the building. "Oh, Jerry's out there bitching and moaning, his usual pleasant self. Scott's standing around, spaced out. And Harold's belching." A chorus of laughter would go up.

I got in Harold's Ford and cranked the seat back. I strapped Harold in with the seat belt. Tiny spots of blood were already seeping through the gauze. Harold moaned.

Jerry leaned into the passenger side of the car. He slapped Harold on the shoulder. "Shake it off, Stalker." When Harold didn't respond, Jerry said, "While you drive, Scott, you might explain to our friend how things

go around here. You might explain the notions of profi-
ciency and skill. You might explain to him the
inevitable consequences should he continue in his pres-
ent course." He smiled as he said this.

I leaned over toward Harold and Jerry. "For once in
your life, Jerry, shut the fuck up." The smile dropped
from Jerry's face. He stood back from the car, hands at
his sides for a moment, then folded his arms across his
belly. I knew what was coming if I hung around any
longer. Harold burst out in tittering laughter. I started
the Ford. It sputtered and coughed.

Once we were out of the parking lot, Harold shouted,
"That was glorious! God damn, Scottie, you showed
him. You sure as hell put him in his—"

"—Shut up, Harold," I said. "I didn't do that for you."

"I don't care. It was great. Did you see the look on his
face? Oh, man! He needs more of that!"

"Shut up, Harold," I said again.

After a moment he said, "You *are* a queer bastard." I
asked him how his arm felt. He grunted, then pulled
the half-smoked cigarette from his shirt pocket. It was
flattened and torn. Shreds of tobacco stuck out, as if it
had exploded, too. "I could really, really go for a smoke
now," he said. "You got any smokes?"

I shook my head. "I'm out."

"My hand is tingling."

"Maybe the doctor will give you something for your
arm. You know, knock out the pain." We pulled to a
stop at a red light, the brakes of Harold's car squeaking.

"I don't want to see a doctor."

"What do you mean, no doctor?"

"Just that," he said. He spat out the window.

The light turned green and I proceeded into the intersection. "We're not going back to the office," I said.

"Hell no," said Harold. "He thinks we're at the hospital. We got time to kill."

"I think I better take you to the hospital."

"I told you, Scottie, no doctor." I shot him a look. For some reason he kept calling me Scottie, which I hated. I'd told him that a dozen times. He must have thought I was questioning his idea, though, because he said, "Look, it's three now. Even if we did go to the hospital, we wouldn't get back to the office by four-thirty, would we? So what's the diff? Jerry won't know. We'll just show up a little after everyone's gone home, and I'll fix my arm up later." After a moment, he said, "Fuck Jerry! That was awesome, Scottie, really awesome."

"I told you, shut up about that."

"Nobody talks shit to his face. That took balls, man. Holy shit!" Harold laughed. "Pull over," he said, pointing at a strip mall. "I want some smokes." I parked in front of a gas station. He fumbled at the door handle with his right hand. "My fingers won't work," he said, giggling. I leaned across to open the door, my forearm brushing his soft, damp belly. He climbed out of the car, which sprang up a couple inches when his weight left it.

"Why don't you want to see a doctor?" I asked. "What are you, Christian Scientist? You've got glass in your arm."

He leaned his big face in the window, and fixed that stare on me. "Whose arm is it?"

"Okay," I said, shrugging my shoulders.

Harold returned with a carton of generic cigarettes, which he tossed onto the dash, saying, "Help yourself." He opened a big bag of Cheetos and started shoveling them into his mouth with his left hand. "You got any pot?" he asked. "You want some? I know a guy."

"I don't think so," I said, shaking my head. All I could do was laugh.

"Okay, then how about some beer? I got money." He stuffed another handful of Cheetos into his mouth. "You know we're not going back to the office. Come on, Scottie."

We drove around aimlessly, sipping forty-ounce Malt Liquor Bulls and listening to classic rock on the radio. Harold's cigarettes were awful, but he was paying me back for all the smokes he'd bummed, and I could have as many as I could stand. So I kept smoking them. Harold kept picking at his arm, and it was bugging me. Every so often I'd ask him if he was sure he didn't want to stop in at the emergency room, but the answer was always the same.

Harold said he wanted to go to the zoo. I couldn't think of anything else to do, so I agreed. In the parking lot I noticed that Harold's right arm was getting worse. The gauze and bandage had soaked through, and it looked like it was starting to congeal. The blood at the ends of the gauze, above the wound, had turned dry and brown. I told him he better cover it up with something or they wouldn't let us in. He took a sweatshirt from the back seat of his car and I helped him put that on.

Harold knew exactly what he wanted to see. "Snakes," he said, his breath stinking of malt liquor.

The reptile tunnel looked like it'd been carved out of rock, though if you tapped the rock it sounded hollow and thin. Walking in there, I couldn't see, but after a few minutes my eyes adjusted and I really felt like I was in a tunnel. It was clammy and cold. Lucky for us, it was feeding day in the tunnel. Snapping turtles chewed on grasshoppers as big as my thumb. Lizards scurried after insects. Crowds of kids were oohing everywhere, faces pressed to the glass observation windows, their parents grimacing or sighing impatiently behind them. Harold charged through them all, heading for his destination.

The window for the boa constrictor was about six feet wide. The cage's setting was tropical. Simulated tree branches and leafy palms hung over ferns and pools of water. We stood close to the glass and watched a white rat move nervously around the floor of the cage, its nose twitching rapidly. Above it, lying on a wide branch, was the boa, thick and still, tan with dark brown spots. I was just about to turn away when Harold said, "Watch this."

The boa dropped off the branch and instantly coiled around the rat. Every time the rat squirmed, the snake tightened another notch. At first the rat moved every few seconds. Then every twenty or thirty seconds. Then it quit moving and the snake lay still for a long time. The rat's eyes bulged in their sockets. The mouth was open and its tongue stuck out, as if it wanted to scream but it couldn't.

"That's a shitty way to go," I said.

Harold belched: *FFFFF.* The reflection of his face in the

glass and dim light was doubly menacing. His eye sockets were dark pools of shadow, his mouth a flat black slit.

We stayed and watched the constrictor. After about twenty minutes it slowly uncoiled itself from the rat, which looked flattened and bent. Then the snake began to ingest the rat, head first. The boa moved slowly, swallowing millimeters at a time. It unhinged its jaw and swallowed more. Harold stared, his face up against the glass. The constrictor's neck ballooned with the shape of the rat. Half the rat was down its throat, the pressed white belly, pink feet, and enormous tail hanging out. Then just the scrawny little feet. Then just the tail, jutting out like an obscene tongue. I tried to imagine swallowing a rat, the feeling of the dry white hair against my throat, the warm body an enormous lump moving slowly down my gullet, into my stomach. I guess snakes don't have a stomach, not like we do. The rat just sits there, bones and brains and shit and all, decomposing.

A young woman wearing the zoo uniform—khaki pants and a green golf shirt—walked up and told us the reptile tunnel closed in ten minutes. A pin on her shirt read, "Ask me about reptiles!"

"How often do snakes eat?" I asked.

"It depends. A snake like Sandy," she said, nodding to the boa, "will digest that rat for a good ten days to two weeks. We won't feed her again until this time next month."

I said, "Jesus."

"Do they eat rabbits?" asked Harold.

"Well, yes, they do," said the woman.

"I knew it," he said, sniggering.

We got a couple more forty-ouncers for the ride home.

It was close to seven o'clock; the sun was hanging above the horizon at that point where it can't be covered by the visor. I drove along Highway 494 quickly, shielding my eyes with one hand, wanting to get back to the parking lot and get away from Harold and this day.

"Is being in the Army anything like what they show you in the movies, Scottie?"

"No," I said. "Why do you keep calling me Scottie?"

"It's like *Star Trek*," he said. "You know, 'Beam me up,' and all that. Scottie was my favorite on the show. The old show."

"My name's Scott."

"In high school we used to call each other names from the show. I had one friend, Derrick, we called him Bones. The exchange student, Yury, he was Chekov, you know?"

"What'd they call you?"

"Jabba."

"Which one was he?"

"Jabba's from *Star Wars*. Jabba the Hut. Because I'm fat," he said. "There weren't any fat people on *Star Trek*." He leaned his head out the window and screamed, "There weren't any fat people on *Star Trek!*"

"You going to be able to drive?" I asked.

"I drank as much as you," he said. He held the bottle up before him. "Three of these ain't shit."

"Yeah, but it's gone to your head."

Harold dropped his beer onto the floor of the car. "Shit," he said.

"Sweaty palms," I said.

"Never you mind my hands, you queer bastard!" he shouted.

I reached for another pack of generic cigarettes. "I

won't make jokes about your hands if you don't call me Scottie."

Harold let loose with a deafening belch; even with the windows down, it stunk like hell. "Man, you showed Jerry today! Yes you did! I loved that!"

I was about to tell him once again to shut up when he punched the dash of his car with his left hand.

"That snake was incredible! Kawerrrrgggghhh!!!" He made a twisting motion in the air with his hands, as if he held the rat.

At first I thought he was just drunk. He kept going on about Jerry and the snake and the rat. He guzzled the rest of his malt liquor and kept babbling. Some of it wasn't making any sense. He started rocking back and forth in his seat as he spoke, smashing his fist into the dash every so often. I thought seriously about pulling over and saying, "Fuck this," but we were just entering Eden Prairie. I ran a couple of stop signs and drove straight to the back of the B&G lot, a few parking spots from my Camaro.

"Let me out of this goddamn car!" he shouted, bouncing up and down, making the Fairmont rock.

"Let yourself out," I said. I left his car running and got out. I'd had more than enough of Harold for a long time.

I almost hit him as I backed my Camaro out of the parking spot. Harold shouted something as I pulled away, heading for the driveway.

I slammed on my brakes when I saw Harold in my rearview mirror. He was kicking one of Jerry's hutches. I put my car in reverse and sped back. By the time I could park and climb out the cage was on the ground, broken up. Harold tore the chicken wire off the wood, blood covering his left arm in gruesome symmetry with his right, which he'd suddenly regained use of. He took rabbit after rabbit from the smashed cage, wringing each neck and then hurling the body across the clearing. Some of the rabbits escaped. A lot of them, actually. There were too many. They were too quick, and they were easily camouflaged in the dirt and brush. I saw a couple nibbling on weeds and grass, and a couple more scurrying for cover as Harold continued thumping and thrashing around. Every rabbit was going to die, I realized, either in Harold's thick hands or stranded in the brush. I knew I couldn't stop Harold—he was too big, and too crazy.

I started with the rabbits on the ground. Most let me pick them up right away; they were used to being handled. They were warm and soft. I picked up as many as I could carry and ran with them to my Camaro, where I dumped them in a pile on my passenger seat. Then I went back for more. When I'd collected as many as I could find on the ground, I ran for the few hutches still left standing. I raced cage-by-cage, grabbing armfuls of rabbits, dodging Harold's clumsy attempts at stopping me as he continued his rampage. I managed four trips, after which there was only one hutch left. Harold got there first, but that was okay. I knew I couldn't save them all.

You Have to Say Something

They met at Café Vienna, a coffee shop near the university. Fran had stopped in during her morning break for a drink. The place was nearly empty, its glossy tables and stout wooden chairs arranged in uncharacteristically neat rows. It was late May, her favorite time to be on campus. The students had cleared out for summer, so parking was easy to find. Restaurants were less crowded. The sidewalks didn't smell like stale beer every morning. Fran ordered her usual: a double vanilla chai, hot. While she waited, she noticed a woman typing on a laptop, nodding along to something on her headphones. Leo Kottke's *Live in Europe* sat on one corner of her table. Fran walked over and asked if she could look at the CD. She'd not heard it.

"Be my guest," the woman said, a bit too loudly. She slid the headphones down around her neck. Silver jewelry encircled her wrists and several fingers. She was deeply tanned and had long, stringy hair in need of a deep conditioning. A bottle blonde, Fran noted.

"You like Kottke?"

"I do," Fran said. "We're working to get him here next spring." She set the case back down on the table. "I work for Convocations over at the university."

"Is that right," the woman said. "Well, it's about time you people started trying to get someone decent. Smashing Pumpkins—what a joke!"

Fran smiled. "That was the Student Concert Committee."

"Whatever." The woman wrote her name and phone number on a rumpled napkin and handed it to Fran. "You call me the minute you know Kottke's coming. I'm there."

"I'll try to remember, Sam." She folded the napkin and put it in her pocket. "My name's Fran."

"I'm glad I ran into you," Sam said. "Now I know who to bribe when I want good seats for a show."

Fran laughed. "You wish."

"Vanilla chai," the coffee server announced.

"My drink," Fran said, nodding to the counter.

"Chai drinker, huh?" Sam made a shoo-shoo motion with her hand. "Off with you, then."

She smiled at Sam on her way out the door. Sam waved; the blue tip of a tattoo peeked out from under the neckline of her dress. Now there's a woman with a history, Fran thought, walking out onto State Street. A woman with stories to tell. People like that intrigued her. They radiated a certain kind of wisdom, a self-assured knowingness. They were open to possibilities. Free to try things. Unafraid to fail. That was a special kind of freedom.

The following Monday, Fran stopped at Café Vienna during her break and there was Sam, tapping away on her laptop with the headphones on. She waved Fran over.

"I got something for you, hon," she said, reaching into her black satchel and producing two boxes of vanilla chai concentrate. "Now you can get your fix at home, too."

Fran smiled, a little embarrassed by the generosity. She'd seen them at the store and knew they were pricey. "Thanks. That's so thoughtful."

"Just a little bribe." Her laugh, Fran noted, was surprisingly sharp and loud.

Sam invited her to sit down and talk. Fran checked her watch.

"Come on," Sam said. "Play hooky."

Fran thought for a moment. Her boss was out of the office that morning. She wasn't expecting any calls or faxes. Nobody would know the difference. "Oh, what the hell," she said, and sat down.

Only it turned out to be an early lunch. Sam, as it happened, could talk and talk. And Fran enjoyed listening. Sam was a returning student, finishing the bachelor's in art history she'd abandoned more than twenty years ago. She was minoring in German, just for kicks. She'd spent the eighties and early nineties living in Madison, Seattle, Boulder. She'd worked in bead shops, record stores, used-clothing boutiques, always for minimum wage. Before returning to school in Indiana, she'd been living in San Francisco with a sixty-year-old painter she thought might finally be The One.

Until she caught him fucking her best friend in the shower.

"That was my big wake-up call," Sam said. "Not that I hadn't been crapped on before. But this guy, Aaron . . ." She shook her head. "It finally hit me, you know? I was forty, permanently single, getting fat. Everything I owned fit in my car. I felt like a joke. I had nothing. No prospects, no money in the bank. Just an address book full of names. All those beautiful people I'd met and left behind because I thought the answer was in the next town."

Sam looked down to her salad, tossing the lettuce over on itself.

"But it wasn't," Fran said.

"It wasn't what?"

"The answer. You never found it."

"Honey, you don't go looking for answers. They come looking for you. It doesn't matter where you are. They just happen." Sam snapped her fingers.

"When you least expect them," Fran said, nodding.

"It's only a question of being open. Things happen every day around you. Most people walk right past them, or through them. Everyone's blind, you know? I'm talking about triggers now. Catalysts. The things you see and hear that prompt change."

"If you're open," Fran repeated, cradling her mug between both hands. "It can happen anytime. Or any-where."

"Or nowhere," said Sam, vacantly, "which is why I came back to West Lafayette."

Fran put her mug back down on the table. "I visited San Francisco once."

"Oh yeah?"

"It was just for a few days. I did an internship one summer at a nonprofit theater in Monterey. I drove up one weekend to visit an old college boyfriend." She took a bite of her sandwich. "I remember now that I left a skirt behind in his apartment. A really beautiful Indian skirt, covered in tiny reflective mirrors and beads. Not expensive. It just had sentimental value."

"And you never got it back."

"No," Fran said. "I called him and asked for it. Even wrote him, I think. But he never responded. Finally I let it go."

"I know the type," Sam grumbled.

Fran smiled. "What would you have done?"

"In the old days I'd of sliced his pecker off and cooked it in hot oil," Sam said, laughing. "But you're looking at the kinder, gentler Samantha Marshall." She sipped her coffee. "Tell me something. Is your hubby like that?"

"Blake? No, he's nothing like that." Fran folded her paper napkin in half, then in half again, pressing each fold tight. "He's not like that at all." She thought about how best to describe Blake, which good quality to name first, but then Sam abruptly switched the topic, as she so frequently did.

"I want to see a movie tonight," Fran said. She stacked the empty dinner plates in the center of the table, silverware on top. The slight chill of the evening air danced around her ankles. She liked to leave windows cracked in spring.

"What do you want to see?" Blake asked.

"That new Meg Ryan film."

"You've Got Mail? Please. How many times can she repeat *Harry Meets Sally?* If you've seen one, you've seen them all."

"I don't care," Fran said, twirling the stem of her wine glass between her fingers. "That's what I want."

"So go."

"I want a date. It's a date film. People who go see a romantic comedy by themselves look like losers. They look worse than losers." She sipped her wine. "They look melancholy and forlorn."

He sighed. "It's a work night, Francesca."

"It's Friday, Blake."

"Right. And if you want me to bowl with you tomorrow, then I've got to work tonight."

She balled up her napkin and tossed it onto the table. "What are you working on?"

"I'm revising that article on Grover Cleveland's agricultural distribution policy."

"The potato thing?"

"The potato thing."

Fran held up her empty wine glass and her balled-up napkin. She looked from one to the other. "Hmm. Love or potatoes? Love or potatoes? It's a Friday night. Guess I'll have to go with the potatoes."

Blake sat back in his chair and laughed. "That's good. I like that one."

Fran leaned forward, pressing her midriff against the table edge. "Come out with me."

They stared at each other for a long moment. Blake lifted an eyebrow. She loved that look, warm and provocative at the same time. But she knew what it meant. She stood and began clearing the dishes from the table.

"I'm glad you called me," Sam said, "though I can't imagine why you wanted to see *that* film." The Tippecanoe Mall parking lot was nearly empty, a sea of asphalt bathed in halogen orange. Fran took a deep breath of the crisp night air. It always cheered her.

"You didn't like it?"

"Meg Ryan is a dumb bitch."

Fran laughed. "I like her. She's so . . . open."

"She's a girly-girl, and you have a crush on her. Everyone does, men and women. Fred Astaire had an insurance policy on his feet? Meg Ryan should insure her pout. That's why you love her."

Fran laughed again. "So why'd you come see it?"

Sam twined her arm through Fran's. "Because you called me."

Fran pulled herself closer. Sam smelled of patchouli. "Thanks."

They strolled slowly along the sidewalk, littered with cigarette butts, empty potato chip bags, and flattened blobs of chewing gum. Fran felt happy. And tired. Her tiredness made her happy.

"Walk me to my car," Sam said.

Fran followed her to a pale yellow Jetta spotted with rust. Sam opened the trunk and took out a brown two-piece outfit, a skirt and matching blouse. Across both pieces were hand-sewn peacocks, elephants, and tigers, with glass beads and gilt stitching.

"It's beautiful," Fran said.

"I can hem it if it's too large," Sam said, handing it to her. "I had to guesstimate."

"You bought this?" Fran said, holding up the outfit. "For me?"

"At Goodwill, sweetheart. Don't lose your popcorn." She squeezed Fran's bare arm and laughed. Her hands felt tough and strong. "Remember the skirt you lost in San Fran? Well, I saw this and figured I could right a wrong."

"Oh, Sam." Fran hugged and thanked her.

On her drive home, however, Fran began to wonder. The skirt—the one she'd lost—hadn't meant much, really. She hadn't thought of it in years; it wasn't a story she often told. Rather, it was the kind of anecdote you shared in order to make a connection with whatever the other person had been telling you. If that would lead Sam to go and buy an outfit for her—well, what harm was there in that?

One June afternoon Fran came home wearing a vintage tuxedo jacket with a daisy in the buttonhole. She found Blake in the living room reading a history journal. A tall stack of them were piled messily on the coffee table.

"Hello, sweet," Fran said.

"How-doo."

He didn't look up. He wore a gray T-shirt and sweat-pants. He hadn't showered or shaved. Pretty standard for summer. If it weren't for his teaching, Fran often joked, he'd forgo personal hygiene altogether.

Fran cleared her throat noisily. He looked up. She playfully modeled the coat, spinning around and showing him the lining.

"Okay," he said. "New coat."

"New old coat," Fran said, brushing a hair from the black sleeve. "It's a '73 Pierre Cardin. Do you like it?"

"Sure," he said. "Where'd you get it?"

"Sam gave it to me. She found it at a used-clothing store."

"And why did she give you a twenty-year-old jacket?"

"She just knows," Fran said, smiling. "She picked up on some vibration."

"She picked up on some old pictures you showed her, or something." He folded a page in the journal and dropped it on the couch beside him. He rubbed the dark circles under his eyes. "You haven't worn clothes like that since we lived in Minneapolis."

"Minneapolis?" Fran said. "Did we live there?"

He smiled. He was willing to play a little. "Five years ago."

Fran slapped her forehead. "Oh god! We forgot to move back to Minneapolis!" She knelt before him and rubbed her hands on his thighs. "Honey, whatever happened to our plan to move back to Minneapolis?"

Blake shook his head. "Has your brother been nagging you again?"

"He gave up ages ago," she said. "But seriously. You said after your book got published you'd look at the market."

"And I did. There were openings in, let's see, South Carolina, Georgia, and Florida. I seem to recall someone vetoing all three."

Fran stuck her tongue out at him, but he smiled.

"Do you still read the listings?" she asked. "Has there been an opening in Minnesota?"

"No."

"No there haven't been any openings, or no you don't read the listings?"

He leaned forward and ran his fingers through her hair, slowly massaging her scalp. She placed her head on his lap. She closed her eyes and concentrated on the feel of his fingers in her hair. The living room windows were open and the air smelled of midsummer: warm, grassy. In mid-June mulberries fell from the trees, staining sidewalks and cars with their purple juice. It was one thing she loved about Indiana. What else did she love? She thought for a moment. Something would come to her.

"I'm happy at Purdue," he said, after a couple of minutes. "This is a good department. They value me here."

"They'd value you in Minnesota."

"That's a very political department. Their last two hires were Marxists."

She nodded her head gently. The issue, she knew, had really been decided years ago. Pressing just made them both grumpy.

His fingers left her hair and moved down her neck to her shoulders. He ran a finger along the collar of her coat.

"Why does that woman give you so many presents?"

"She likes me."

"I know," he said. "But doesn't it strike you as odd? She gives you something every time she sees you. It doesn't seem right."

She drew her lips in and held her breath a long moment. "It doesn't mean what you think," she said.

She stood and walked slowly from the room.

Fran had to admit she liked receiving gifts. And the gifts kept coming, all throughout that summer and fall. Sam didn't just give her anything; each gift had its place. Some, like the Indian skirt, were in response to something particular. Others, like the tuxedo jacket, showed how perceptive she could be.

If Sam bought her a lot of gifts, at least Fran took heart in knowing that she never spent a lot of money. Things were always on sale, or used. But Blake was right: there were so many of them, and they came so frequently. Sometimes it was small—a box of tea, or a paperweight carved out of sandstone. Other times it was whole out-fits, or expensive-looking cut glass bowls. Sam always claimed she'd gotten the items for a song, and that Fran shouldn't worry about it. But Fran did wonder about the money. She knew Sam was a part-time student, working twenty hours a week at an East Asian imports shop (where she could get batik and sandalwood incense—Fran's favorite—at cost). There was no savings account. The gifts were coming right out of Sam's pay-checks. Out of rent money. Or the grocery budget.

She began to feel uncomfortable. Guilty, even, that this woman would spend so much time and money on her. Privilege her so. She wondered if it were possible for Sam to be in her presence without some kind of offering. Was it just her, or did Sam do this for everyone she liked? She made up her mind to have a word with Sam, to be honest and direct about the matter.

But then Sam showed up with a smile on her face, a joke to tell, and a little something wrapped up for her. And

Fran's resolve melted away. It was so easy to give in, to accept the gifts in the spirit which, Fran believed, Sam intended them. Such giving was real; it was genuine and selfless. She chose gifts for *you*, for the person she saw and understood. Her gifts spoke like a partner in dialogue. *I know you. I know who you are, who you want to become.*

And then there was the search itself. Sam had a sixth sense for shopping; not only did she know every bargain shop and discount den in Indy, she knew of rummage sales in Rensselaer, auctions in Attica, and clear-outs in Crawfordsville. Half the fun was listening to Sam tell you how she found the gift. Every dimension of the offering—from the moment Sam found it to the moment she placed it in your hands—had its own measurable quality. Sam herself defined it as a holistic process. Everyone benefited.

And so when Sam invited Fran to join her on a weekend shopping spree in Indianapolis, Fran was eager to go. She'd accompanied Sam as she poked through the pawn shops and boutiques of Lafayette; it would be another experience to see her in action at a big flea market, to see how she selected the things she bought. Yet Fran felt a bit uneasy about accompanying her, about encouraging the spending. The day before the flea market she still hadn't responded to Sam's invitation. She asked Blake for advice.

"Don't go," he said, chopping vegetables for a stir fry. "I can't believe you don't see what's going on. She's buying your friendship. She's trying to win you over with presents."

"Why?"

"She's probably insecure, afraid she can't otherwise impress you."

"No, not Sam. It's not that."

He pushed a slice of carrot her way. She took it up and bit it.

"Well then, what do you make of it?" Blake stood in the kitchen in his running clothes. His cheeks and neck were still flushed from his run. He liked to come home and do things around the house before showering. Wash dishes. Sort the recycling. Prepare dinner. She found it sexy, in a way. Sometimes she had him make love to her right as he came in the door, all sweaty and hot. Then they'd shower together. They hadn't done that in some time. Lately they'd been making love on weekend mornings, if then.

"She's just generous," Fran said. "And her gifts are so . . . thoughtful." She told him how, after she'd complained about insects biting her at an outdoor concert, Sam had given her a bottle of all-natural lemongrass bug spray. Then there was the time Sam dropped off an entire plate of pork tamales, just because Fran had mentioned a certain meal she and Blake remembered fondly from their honeymoon in Mexico, five years ago.

"You remember those," Fran told Blake.

"Which, the street vendor's, or Sam's?"

Fran reached across the table and took another carrot slice. "Both."

"I do," he said, playfully slapping the back of her hand. "Sam is a good cook. But it doesn't remove the sense of entrapment."

"That's too strong a word."

"No, it isn't. Not if she's purchasing your time and attention with gifts."

"Maybe I want to go to this flea market in Indy. Is that still entrapment?"

"I don't know. The point is, you're on the fence. And that's because a little part of you knows something is wrong." He took the wok down from its hook on the kitchen wall and put it on the stove top. A dozen blue-white fingers of gas appeared beneath it. "Never mind that you'd already made a date to go hiking with your husband," he added, dumping the cut vegetables into the wok.

Fran ran a finger along the edge of the table. "Pardon me if this trip coincides with your self-appointed day off from researching the great potato crop of 1872."

"Whoa!" Blake said, laughing. "Measurable sarcasm!"

"Well, come on. You know what I'm talking about."

It was an old argument between them, and not one Fran was particularly interested in reopening. She was glad, then, when Blake shrugged his shoulders and said, "I'm just razzing you. Go to Indy, if you want."

"Give me a carrot," she said. "It's a thinking food."

On the hour-long drive down, Sam talked about her new love interest. Blake might know him, she said. He was a graduate student in history, working on a Ph.D. in nineteenth-century economic policy. He was her age, sported a Hemingway beard, and had an awesome collection of concert T-shirts.

"Which makes sense," Sam said, "given that he manages the record store across the street from my shop, which is where I met him."

Fran thought for a moment. "Tim Zellar?"

"Yes!" Sam said, pounding the steering wheel. "You know him?"

"Blake knows him," Fran said. "A former student."

"Nothing former about him," Sam said. "He and I, we believe in life-long education. Permanent student status. Though I guess he's nearly finished with his dissertation."

Fran cleared her throat, searching for the most diplomatic language she could find. "He's been nearly completed for the entire five years we've lived in West Lafayette. He was one of Blake's first doctoral candidates. He ran out of funding a couple years ago and really raised a stink about not getting a visiting instructor's position."

"So he and Blake don't get along?"

"He and Blake don't get along."

"Well, he did complain about tightwads in the department."

For a long moment, Fran was quiet. She knew she ought to deny the charge. Instead, she laughed.

Sam turned to look at her, then punched her lightly on the arm. "I like you, girly-girl."

In truth, Fran was glad to have a day away from Blake. He always became testy in early August. While she knew he loved teaching, he also looked at it as a burden that cut into his research. And no matter how much he'd accomplished in a summer, it was never enough. When a school term began, he only became more protective of his time. Fran pressed a fingernail into the naugahyde door panel. They had no "couple's time." Only time off the clock from his work that he chose to spend with her. She was a research widow. A second thought.

The flea market occupied a corner of an enormous parking lot near a strip mall in central Indianapolis. Across the street was a park with a lake and a thick stand of trees crowned in the robust green of summer. It was a warm, bright August day. The sun felt good on Fran's bare shoulders.

For a time, she followed Sam as she made her way slowly up and down the rows. Fran watched her friend, noted the kinds of knick-knacks she was picking up and putting down. But she soon let herself drift a table away, then two, before finally giving up. The market just didn't interest her. She wasn't a collector. It took a lot of time and energy to look through all the junk spread out on these tables. You had to have an eye for it, a sense of what you wanted. Otherwise, it was all just crap. Crap spread out in a parking lot. Big deal.

Fran found herself standing on the edge of the market, staring across the busy avenue at the park, watching a young man with a goatee throw a Frisbee for his dog. The dog, a golden retriever with a rich, glossy coat, leapt high into the air to snatch the Frisbee in its mouth. Then it landed, turned around, and sprinted back to its master. Each time the dog returned, the man gave it a big hug. The dog's enormous pink tongue bobbed in the heat. Then the man stood and tossed the Frisbee again.

Blake had decided to go hiking at Turkey Run without her. A day off was a day off, he said. Use it or lose it. Tomorrow, a Sunday, would be spent in his office. She would be free to do anything. Or nothing. Anything and nothing.

She felt a tug at her shirtsleeve. She turned to find Sam beside her, holding out a small oil painting encased beneath glass and surrounded by an ornate gold frame. It looked very old. And expensive.

"What do you think?"

"It's beautiful," Fran said.

"Check out the tree," Sam said, tapping the glass with a fingertip.

"A white birch." The tree stood on a narrow promontory overlooking a lakeshore, its slender branches leaning out over the still water. The quality of detail in the small painting was remarkable. Papery, white bark curled away from the tree trunk. Leaves danced on the lake's surface. A deep blue sky resonated behind it all.

Sam handed the painting to Fran.

"Oh, no," Fran said. "You couldn't."

"It's your favorite tree," Sam said. "Plus, for what it's worth, it's a John K. Chandler. The dealer doesn't know shit about Depression-era landscape miniatures, or the price would be double what it is. Was."

Fran bit her lower lip. She had told Sam, ages ago, that her favorite tree was the white birch. They were rare in central Indiana, but plentiful in northern Minnesota, where she'd grown up. She and her brother used to write poems to each other on the bark.

"No," Fran said, shaking her head. "I can't. This looks . . . I mean, it's expensive, isn't it?"

"You'd think. But I got it for a song. Like I said, the dealer doesn't know shit."

"No, Sam, seriously . . ."

She handed Fran a plastic bag with bubble wrap wadded up inside. "Take a good look, then wrap it up and tuck it away in the Jetta."

"Why do you do this?" Fran said.

"Do what?"

"Why do you give me all these gifts?"

Sam scowled and put a hand on her hip. "What do you mean, why?"

"I'm beginning to feel uncomfortable," Fran said, softly.

Sam shook her head slowly. "I get this from everybody sooner or later." She ran a hand over her face. "You want to know what my deal is, where I'm coming from, what's attached to it, right? Well, the answer is *nada*. Don't worry about it. I give gifts because it's who I am. It's part of my personality. It's how I express myself." A moment later, she added, "I thought you understood that."

"I do understand, but . . . ," Fran began.

Sam cut her off with a sharp wave of the hand. "Hey, it's my prerogative, isn't it? I decide what to do with my money. Why can't you just accept it?"

"I . . ." But Fran didn't know what to say.

"Meet you at the car in fifteen," Sam said, handing Fran the keys. Then she turned and walked back into the market.

Fran waited a minute, trying to clear her head. She set the painting on the corner of a nearby table and then took the bubble wrap from the bag. As she did so, a white scrap of paper fell from the wrap and was quickly blown out into an aisle of the market. A white-haired man wearing a beautiful felt fedora stepped on the paper, then picked it up. He looked at it before handing it back to her.

"Here's your receipt," he said. He looked down at the painting on the table. "There's another market this weekend out near Speedway. You'll find plenty of those boxed landscapes there. Probably pay a bit less, too, if you don't mind my saying."

She looked at the painting. Part of the frame was chipped, revealing a bit of raw wood.

"But it's a John K. Chandler," she said.

He nodded. "Still, I'd never pay over two hundred for anything he did."

She unfolded the receipt, read it over carefully, and stuck it in her jeans pocket. "Oh, Lord," she said, rubbing her brow.

"I hope you don't think me rude," the man said. "But when you see a dealer take someone like that, you have to say something."

Fran looked up at the man. He had warm blue eyes and a handsome nose. She smiled.

"No," she said. "Thank you. You're very helpful."

He raised a finger to the brim of his fedora, then walked slowly off.

She tossed the bag and bubble wrap into a garbage can. Then she picked up the painting and walked into the market.

Fran sat at a window table of Café Vienna, laughing as she read *The Purdue Exponent's* review of *La Triviata*. Apparently a "cool light show" and "a tenor on par with Alanis" was enough to wow the peanut gallery. And it might, if you didn't know opera from Oprah.

Personally, she'd thought the performance mediocre. It was a touring group, and they'd sounded tired. From the business end, however, things couldn't have been better. Elliott Hall had sold out on the Friday night before October break. Fran's boss had already told her to book the troupe again for next season.

Fran fingered the envelope on the tabletop. She looked up at the clock. Twenty past. She'd give Sam another ten minutes.

Sam entered in a full-length leather coat, a provocative red. Fran stood and waved. She breathed in Sam's patchouli as they hugged.

"Great coat," said Fran. "Is it leather?"

"Are you joking?" She dropped the coat in a pile beneath the picture window. They went to the counter together to order drinks, then returned to the table and chatted comfortably, catching each other up. Sam would be finishing her B.A. in December—a bit earlier than expected. She and Tim would be moving in together soon. Things looked good. Real good.

"I'm glad," Fran said. "I know you've been wanting someone steady."

"Ah, don't hide it. You and Blake think Tim's a turdball."

Fran reddened. "Blake, maybe."

"Anyhoo, what diff is it to you guys? You don't have to smell his farts."

Fran laughed then, good and hard. She was glad for it. She sipped her chai.

"So how is the Blakester?"

"He's fine," Fran said. "He got a sabbatical for next year."

"A whole year off?" Sam said, leaning forward.

"Cool! Where you gonna go? Let me guess: Minneapolis. No, Hawaii. I give up."

Fran ran a finger around the rim of her mug. "He wants to stay in town. Be near the library."

Sam sat back in her chair. "Oh. Okay."

"He's working on a new book," Fran said, shrugging her shoulders. "Moving around gets him all flustered."

"So *you* take the year off. Leave him home to stew in his juices. He won't even miss you."

Fran looked up to meet Sam's steel-steady gray eyes. The words had sounded harsh, though Fran thought she detected a slight, almost indefinable gentleness behind them. A loving nudge. Fran dropped her gaze back to her mug.

"I'm glad you returned my phone call."

"Well, I couldn't blow you off forever."

"It seemed like you were going to."

"Oh," Sam said, pouting playfully. "I can play hard-to-get."

"I want to apologize. I think you know I—"

"—Forget it," Sam interrupted. "Don't pick open old scars."

"Please," Fran said, holding a hand up. "Let me have my say, okay?"

Sam rolled her eyes but gestured for Fran to continue.

"I know you're angry with me. What I did hurt you, I know that. I hope you remember what I said when I gave you that money back, because I still mean it." She paused to take a breath. She'd promised herself not to get distracted in overanalyzing the ugly scene in Indy that day.

"But I don't want to talk about August," she said. "I want to talk about now."

"Now?"

"I'm hoping we can see each other again. Sort of start over. I brought you a peace offering." She pushed the white envelope across the table to Sam.

Sam looked at it for a moment, then picked it up and opened the flap. She looked inside for several seconds, then closed her eyes and shook her head.

"First row balcony for Kottke," Fran said.

Sam set the envelope down and pushed it to the middle of the table with the tip of her index finger. "I can't accept them."

"Don't worry," Fran said quickly. "I didn't pay a dime for them. They're comps. I won them in an office pool. I want you and Tim to go."

"No," Sam said, shaking her head. "The show's in February. I won't be here."

"You won't?"

"Tim and I are moving to Brooklyn right after I graduate. I'm interning at the MOMA. Can you believe it? That asswipe, Aaron, the painter in San Fran? Turns out he knows a guy."

"Oh," Fran said, looking at the envelope. "Congratulations."

"Well, it ain't gonna pay the bills," Sam said, flatly. "I'll be moonlighting for a while. But it's a start." She laughed. "You know, you were right about one thing. Tim won't ever finish that Ph.D. Only took him about three minutes to sign on to my plan."

"Well, that's great," Fran said.

"It is. You know I've been chomping at the bit to get the fuck out of this town, no offense to stranded bystanders." Sam rapped the table top with her knuckles. "But let me set you straight about last August, 'cause I want to get this over with real quick. Yes, you pissed me off. Yes, that's why I didn't return your calls. No, I won't hold it against you forever. If you want, we can hang out. I won't give you any gifts," she said, pushing the envelope all the way across the table, "and you won't, either. Agreed?"

She held a hand out. Fran took it. They shook.

When they left the café a half hour later, she and Sam embraced on the street. They promised to call each other soon. Fran waited to see Sam drive off, and waved after her. Then she turned and walked slowly along State Street. It was chilly for mid-October, but there was no breeze. All around her she smelled crisp, dry leaves and the promise of the coming frost. She thought of her brother in Minneapolis. Up there, he'd told her on the phone the other night, the leaves were all down. They'd had their first frost. Predictions were for a heavy snowfall. He'd invited Fran and Blake to visit for Christmas. She hadn't mentioned it to Blake yet. She could guess his response.

But she could go. She could leave Blake.

At least for a while.

She didn't notice she'd missed her usual turn until she reached the corner of State and Oval. Her second-story office in Stewart Center was just a half-block behind, on the opposite side of the undergrad library. But she lingered, watching a small group of students assembled on the lawn of the Memorial Mall, across the street. They were shouting about something, holding up placards and cheering. They seemed so sure of themselves, or whatever cause it was they believed in. Their energy and conviction attracted her, so she stared a minute longer.

The Hillside Slasher

Dear Mr. Davies,

I trust you remember who I am. If you do not, briefly glance at the attached news article from the *Duluth Tribune*, and you will certainly recall what I did to you. And you will almost certainly recall, in an instant, that you do not know why I ever did such a thing. You asked me, when you came to see me in the hospital the day after the incident, why a man my age would behave in such a manner, and if I had ever done this kind of thing before. I would not answer your questions then, much to your chagrin. You called me a "doddering old fool" and accused me of senility. You always did have a sharp tongue, Mr. Davies.

Now that I have passed from this life I believe I can finally offer you suitable answers to your questions, and an explanation of why I could not answer them in 1988. That is the purpose of this letter, which has been delivered to you by my son Ernest, the executor of my last will and testament.

In order for me to fully explain why I did what I did, I think you need to understand something about me, something about my late wife, and something about the motives behind the kind of crimes we did. It is the only way I can answer you.

For me, it started during the heat wave of the summer of 1985. My wife, Kate, and I were sitting on the front porch of our house, sipping drinks and talking, as we often did at night after we'd done our work for the day. We lived in an old brownstone duplex on Fifth Street, which we'd purchased and renovated in the early sixties. We rented the other half out to married couples, mostly, so we never had too much trouble. The house was lovely, perched high on the hill overlooking Lake Superior. On warm summer nights we could watch the boat traffic around the port. We'd sit side by side in our folding lawn chairs, me with my bad leg stretched out and resting comfortably, cane at my side. Kate was limber and lean to the day she died, and so she'd lift her bare feet up onto the porch railing, wiggling her toes in the summer breeze.

Kate asked me that night to tell her a secret, something I'd never told her before. She liked those kinds of questions. She asked them regularly, though not often. You see, Kate liked to be surprised. For most of my life I resented her questions. Understood her to be a probe, a nose. But in the later years of our marriage I came to understand that, for Kate, life was a continuous and unsolvable mystery, and it was the relationships we humans form along the way that are the keys to unlocking as much of the mystery as we can. She liked to ask people to confess secrets because she learned a little something each time someone confessed. And, having confessed, you learned a little something, too.

I have only realized that in hindsight. Unfortunately I never got the chance to tell Kate I finally understood why she was always asking people odd questions. Perhaps she had to die before I could understand. Now I wish I'd answered more of her questions, answered more of them honestly. I'm ready for Kate now. But for most of my life, and most of my married life, I lived in a kind of shell, separate from everyone and everything around me. I didn't really understand why at the time but now I can tell you I was scared and lonely.

People say that when you get old, you lose your inhibitions.

It's true.

So I didn't know it at the time, but on that hot July night back in 1985 Kate and I were really starting something. We'd been married thirty-eight years. We'd raised two boys, one of whom died in Vietnam, God rest his soul. The other, Ernest, is a lawyer down in Minneapolis. I retired from teaching geometry in the Duluth Public Schools in June of 1980, and spent the first five years of my retirement as a volunteer, teaching adult literacy and working for the DFL party here in Duluth.

When Kate asked me to tell her a secret that night, I grumbled. I didn't think I had any left that I wanted to tell her. But she insisted, so I told her that I'd had a serious crush on Evie Johnston, our neighbor from three doors down. Evie had moved to Florida a couple of months before, after her husband, David, passed away.

He had a stroke while driving his car between the Twin Cities and Duluth and had crossed the median from the northbound to the southbound lane of I-35 and collided head-on with a tractor-trailer, killing the driver of the tractor, too. But for some twenty-odd years we'd lived on the same block and had seen each other, and for twenty-odd years I'd watched the woman's figure ripen and mature like fruit, and I had wanted to pick that apple more than once.

"Oh, now, that's completely obvious," Kate said, in that pepper-sharp voice of hers. "Any fool knew that. With the way you'd stare at her during block picnics or when she was bent over, weeding that little flower garden by their front steps? Come on, George, tell me a *real* secret."

I was a little surprised and taken aback by Kate's reaction. First, that she didn't seem the least bit bothered by my confession. She and Evie had been best friends, practically. Second, that she knew. That I was so obvious. That meant Kate probably knew that I had lusted after countless other women, which was true. I am a lusty man by nature.

These realizations gave me the courage to say what I said next.

"I saw your sister naked before I saw you naked."

There was a long pause. I thought, again, I might have offended her. She was close to her sister. I could see Kate's slender, lined face in the bright moonlight of that night, and it was calm for a long moment. She brought a hand to her face and brushed a strand of her thick, gray hair back behind her ears. Then she bent forward on the porch chair, over her knees, and burst out laughing so loud I was afraid she'd wake up the whole neighborhood, which I instantly realized was a silly idea because it was eleven o'clock on the hottest night of the year, and it was a Friday to boot, and if I looked up and down the block I could see most of our neighbors sitting out on their porches, drinking and talking just like Kate and I were.

"You saw Jane naked? Before we were married? When?"

I proceeded to tell Kate something funny and true, something that neither I nor Jane had ever told anyone, and that was about a summer night in 1946 in Minneapolis. I'd just returned from Europe and I was in the Twin Cities visiting an Army buddy, Bernie Giles. Bernie was a real crazy guy and he had some money, too. I'd served as a cook in Europe. I couldn't fight on account of my one bad leg. Bernie had gotten himself a position on the supply line. He was the guy responsible for moving foodstuffs from the ports in France right up to the front lines, where I was. Bernie had the knack for that kind of job. He was real friendly with everyone, a smooth talker. A slick, I guess. But he could turn on that charm and make you feel like if you would just do this one favor for him you'd be his best friend. And he made you want to be his friend. Bernie could weasel what he wanted out of just about anyone. He could be a real pain in the neck now that I think about it, but his parties were always a lot of fun because you knew there'd be loads of women and loads of booze.

I don't remember a whole lot of that one particular party before 3 A.M. Not that I was so drunk, though I was a bit drunk, just that it was a pretty ordinary party until somebody mentioned something about a strip poker party in the bedroom. I wandered over that way to check it out and found Bernie in the doorway.

"Georgie," he said, smiling and grabbing my arm. He had a round but charismatic face, and his brown eyes twinkled with intensity. He pulled me in the room. "Just the guy we were looking for. We needed a fourth."

Sitting there on the floor of the bedroom, three sheets to the wind, were Jane and another girl, a cousin of Bernie's, I think. Jane was the prettier of the two, a tall brunette, lean and dolled up with a fancy hairdo and makeup. She'd drawn a black line up the backs of her calves because there was the nylon shortage then. Oh, she was a real dish. The other girl—I can't remember her name now—was more plain-looking, but as the game got underway I realized she was a sly little thing who spoke out of the side of her mouth and cast these looks at you where she narrowed her eyes and stared, catlike.

Well, I was pretty glad I'd stumbled into that room. Right away we were all laughing and joking. Everyone was drunk, and these girls were wild, I could tell that. So I grabbed the cards and dealt the first hand. I wanted to get on with the game because I wanted to see Jane naked. I wanted to see her pull that black sweater over her pretty head and show me her breasts. I'd been alone a long time. And this was a north country girl with hazel eyes and clear skin. We'll just leave it at that.

I was the first to become naked. I've never been good at cards, and I was drunk enough that I probably missed all kinds of possible hands staring me in the face. We all had articles of clothing in a pile before us, but it was me who finally had nothing left but his boxer shorts on and I lost those to Jane and that was it. I had to stand up, pull down my shorts, and then try to win them back. I was embarrassed, to be sure, but then again we were all drunk and laughing and those girls were having a good time.

Jane was the next to lose. She was down to her slip and her bra. I thought she'd take off her slip and play with her bra and panties on, but some odd sense of modesty or outright forwardness led her to choose to remove her bra, a big thing with lots of straps and hooks. She smiled and turned her back to me and asked me to help unfasten it from behind. Oh Lord, I thought, I'm naked and this gorgeous woman just asked me to unfasten her bra! My fingers trembled as I touched the skin on this strange woman's back. I slipped my clumsy fingers underneath the elastic and unhooked three eye-and-hook fasteners and she said "Thank you" and with her back still toward me slipped one strap off her shoulder, then the other. I was just about out of my mind, watching the tight, defined muscles move under the skin of her back, her shoulder blades moving smoothly.

She turned around and, well, I couldn't help it, I took a good long look at her breasts. They were beautiful breasts, sure, but the first thing that popped into my head was how sore they looked. Red indentations ran along the curves and undersides of her breasts, the impression of bra on flesh. Two or three little black hairs stood out from her nipples. It was a strange moment. I don't know, Mr. Davies. Maybe I am a prig, like my wife often used to say.

I don't remember how long we played, but everyone was, at one point or another, completely naked. They even had me streak out into the street at one point because I had lost again and didn't have a shred of clothing to my name. And the whole time we kept laughing and joking and drinking and I kept looking at Jane, wanting her desperately. I wasn't all that interested in the cat-eye girl, and anyway it was pretty obvious that she and Bernie had something going on. So it was no surprise that, after an hour or two, Bernie and his cat-girl cousin called it a game and left the room, clutching their clothes to their naked bodies.

I was suddenly alone with Jane, and we were both absolutely naked.

"What are we going to do now?" she asked. It was the voice of a young lady who had suddenly found herself in a very odd situation: drunk, naked, alone with a horny young serviceman. Scared.

I know what a lot of guys would have done, and believe me, those thoughts careened through my head. I asked her, "Should I stay or should I go?"

She lowered her chin. I got another good look at her body. Her breasts looked smooth and warm now, inviting. Oh, she was beautiful.

"I think you should go."

I began gathering my clothes and wished Jane a good night. A million things rushed through my mind in those minutes. All kinds of voices telling me what to do or what not to do, that I was a saint, a fool, a coward. I had just about finished dressing and was hobbling my way for the door to leave her alone to dress when she spoke.

"Wait," Jane said. "Come here." She was still topless, but she had her panties and her skirt back on. I walked tentatively toward her and she stood on her tiptoes and put both of her hands on the back of my head and kissed me full on the lips. The soft weight of her warm bosom pressed up against my chest. I put my hand on the small of her back.

It was a drunken kiss, a deep, wet, gin-soaked kiss, but I have never forgotten it or the electricity I felt after she finally pulled away. It was like I'd been stung by a live wire, and the jolt had cleared my head of its fuzziness, of the drunken stupor I'd lapsed into. I suddenly felt incredibly awake, incredibly alive, incredibly lonely.

"That's for being a nice guy," Jane said, turning away. "Now you should go."

I didn't see her again until I was dating Kate up in Duluth. You can imagine the heart-stopping surprise Jane and I got when we were introduced to each other.

I told Kate that story that night and she laughed and laughed her way through it, which made me feel good. I was glad I'd had the guts to tell her, glad she'd taken it in such good spirits, glad I'd never done anything on the night back in '46 to regret. It was funny that Jane had never told Kate. Although I'd never asked, I'd just assumed that at some point the sisters had shared that story. Jane and I never talked about it except once, and that was on my wedding night. Jane and I danced a waltz at the reception in the church basement. She leaned up and whispered something about it into my ear and from that moment on Jane and I were great friends. We both remembered, both thought it harmless and funny, and both enjoyed the irony of me marrying her older sister.

I realize that this is a rather lengthy digression, Mr. Davies, but I hope you can bear with me. I am an old man and filled with memories and I am no longer afraid or ashamed to talk about any number of things which, when I was your age, I could only keep locked up in my heart.

But back to that night in 1985. When I had finished telling my story to Kate, it was Kate's turn to tell me a secret. And what she told me that night on our porch changed everything—changed the way I viewed my wife, changed our marriage, and changed me.

"I am the Hillside Slasher," she said.

I didn't believe her, and I told her so. I told her that was the most ludicrous thing I'd ever heard, and that I would appreciate it if she would be honest and tell me something true, because I had just told her a secret, a true secret, and it hadn't exactly been easy. I'd been a little afraid, as I mentioned.

Kate stood up and walked into the house without saying anything. I thought she might be mad. And I slipped into an old routine then, which means that I sat right there on the porch, silent and unmoving. I was not going to follow my wife and ask her if she was angry, because I never did that. If she were angry, typically I would wait for her to cool down and then she would approach me and then she would explain to me why she was mad and what it was that I had done that had upset her. By then we'd been married, as I mentioned, thirty-eight years, and I knew most of it by heart. You might call it the geometry of love, the set of angles and relationships that defined the boundaries and size of our relationship. At least, that's how I came to think of it, over time.

Kate came back out onto the porch and placed a manila folder and a penlight in my lap and then sat back down in her chair. She didn't say anything, so I opened the folder, turned on the penlight, and began reading its contents. They were all clippings from the *Duluth Tribune,* all about the Hillside Slasher, as people were calling the person. Places. Dates. Who'd been hit.

"This doesn't prove anything," I said, thumbing through them.

"Don't mess them up. They're in chronological order," Kate said.

I repeated my statement.

Kate cleared her throat and began reeling off a list of the incidents. First time the Slasher (the *Tribune* wasn't calling the person by that name yet then) struck: May fourth, outside 503 Sixth Avenue East. Ford Thunderbird. Right rear tire. Then, May seventh. Two cars on the 1700 block of Superior Street. A Plymouth Fury and a brand-new Ford Mustang. May seventeenth, six cars in a four block area near the courthouse. And on. Dates. Locations. Make and model of the vehicle. In all, thirty-seven vehicles to date. The last tire slashing had occurred four nights ago. It made the front page because it was in Lakeside.

> The Hillside Slasher has struck again, but this time outside of his usual central Duluth stomping grounds. Mr. Arnold J. Dawson, of 4101 McCulloch,

woke to find the right rear tire of his 1982 Toyota Starlet flat. A subsequent call to police and a visit by an officer confirmed Mr. Dawson's fears: the Slasher had struck.

Police spokeswoman Della C. Gentry said that the vandalism was most definitely the work of the Hillside Slasher. Police were able to identify the distinctive style or method the Slasher uses to puncture the tires. And, as always, a note was tucked under the windshield wiper of the vehicle.

And, as has been the case all summer, police refused to divulge the text of the note.

"The Duluth Police understand and acknowledge the public's wish to know more about the Hillside Slasher," Gentry said from downtown Police headquarters. "But if we release the text of this note we are afraid there will be a rash of 'copy-cat' tire slashings. More than there already have been, I should say." Such occurrences would only complicate Police efforts to apprehend the real Slasher, Gentry said, adding that, when the time was right, all of the information about the Hillside Slasher would be released.

Do the Police have plans to release this information and solicit help from the greater public at large? Some say Police Chief Tony McDermott won't make that move because it would be taken as yet another example of his department's inefficiency and inability to solve or reduce crime in the Port City.

"This whole investigation is a joke," said Town Council member Clarence Davies (IR). "McDermott can't catch a pathetic vandal who slashes tires and leaves some stupid note. How can we trust police to serve and protect our children and families?" Davies and others on the Council have called for McDermott's resignation.

Anyone with information about the Slasher should call the Duluth Police department. There is a $500 reward for anyone with information that will lead to the arrest and conviction of the Hillside Slasher.

Police also urge any subsequent victims of the Slasher to call them immediately and not to release the text of the note to the media, as that could compromise the now "substantial" case the police have against the Slasher.

To date, the Slasher is responsible for an estimated $2,775 worth of damage to thirty-seven vehicles' tires in the city of Duluth.

I looked up after reading that article to find my wife watching me, a big smile on her lips. Something flashed in the bright moonlight and I saw that she cradled a four-inch butcher knife in her lap.

"Want to go for a ride, George?"

I burst out laughing at that because the whole thing seemed so strange and absurd, and yet it was becoming apparent that Kate was serious and in earnest.

Kate had always been fond of evening walks. Any time of the year. She often liked to walk around the neighborhood before coming to bed. Up until 1973 or so, when I had to get my cane and walking on my bad leg became increasingly painful, I would walk with her, sometimes, and we would talk about all kinds of things, about my classes that year at Duluth East or her work with the DFL. She spent a lot of time traveling down to the state capital and back, lobbying legislators and participating in demonstrations and voter registration drives, and so on. Kate was always very active, and never seemed to run out of zeal or energy. But after '73 I couldn't walk more than a block or two without measurable discomfort, and so Kate had taken these walks alone at night.

I saw that there was at least a logistical possibility that my wife was the Hillside Slasher. But I still could not believe it.

We got in our car and Kate drove up Mesaba Avenue, then over by the UMD campus. She was feeling experimental, she said. She'd probably slashed too many in too small an area too fast. There were plenty of others she could hit, who deserved to be hit. And the police had really beefed up the patrols in central Duluth. She'd had to get pretty sneaky and pretty quick about the whole thing.

"How long can it take to slash a tire?" I asked.

"That? Five seconds. I'm talking about the notes. I used to write each one of them by hand, on the hood of the car. Each note was more or less the same, but writing it on the spot made the action more personal. It gave each slashing its own unique signature, so to speak."

"None of this makes one damn bit of sense," I grumbled.

"It wouldn't, to you," Kate said.

No, it didn't make any sense to me then—not the slashings, and certainly not the idea that each one was its own unique event. It was crazy. Stupid. But then I recalled how she'd been able, just minutes before, to recite, in order, each of the thirty-seven cars she had allegedly vandalized, including the date, the make and model, and the approximate street address. Not every slashing had been reported in the paper. And not every article contained all of that information for every slashing. So there had to be something personal about it.

And then, a moment later, I thought that if she really was the Hillside Slasher—and I was beginning to think that she was—then I was fast on my way to becoming an accomplice. Or was it just a hoax, an elaborate joke she was playing on me for some odd reason? Kate had been known to do that from time to time.

But if she were the Slasher and if I were to become an accomplice, and if we were to get caught and suddenly had to pay $2,775 in damages, plus court costs, plus attorney's fees?

I would have had to pay them either way.

Kate tossed me a stack of paper, small sheets cut into two-by-three rectangles, with a thick rubber band holding them together. The sheet on top contained this message, written in crude, block-style capital letters:

YOU SET US BACK A MILE BUT NOW IT IS YOUR TURN. THIS ONE'S FOR THE GIPPER.

"Those are photocopies," Kate said. I checked them. They were all identical. "Copies save me time."

"This is the note you leave under the wipers?" I asked. "I don't get it."

"I sign each one 'Fritz.'"

It took me a minute, but then I put it together. The Gipper. Fritz.

"This is a political act?"

"Essentially, yes." She laughed. The scope and implications of her campaign began to dawn on me.

"These are not random victims."

"No, not exactly," Kate said. "But it's not like I'm going down the IR membership list, though I've hit a few here and there."

"Ernie Andersen."

"Yup."

"Ted Johnson."

She giggled. "Wasn't that good?"

I laughed. "I have to admit a little voice was laughing in my head when I read about that in the paper. That aisle-flopping weasel. But why haven't the police figured this out? It seems a little too obvious."

"Not every victim is an IR member, and not everyone is even necessarily Republican. Some are just marginal supporters, or cross-over voters."

"The worst kind."

"Right," she said, reaching over and patting my hand.

"So how do you know who is who?"

She took a pocket-sized spiral notebook from her purse and handed it to me. Inside it were street addresses. No names. Just hundreds of street addresses, all written in my wife's neat, flowing cursive. Several addresses were crossed out.

"All the houses in the Duluth area that had any kind of Republican paraphernalia displayed during last fall's election season. Signs in the yard, bumper stickers in the window."

"You walked around noting this?"

"Well, I was driving all over the place delivering signs for Mondale, for Duegell, for Karp, for them all. You know. I did that quite a bit."

"Yes, you did," I recalled.

"And every time I passed a house with a Republican sign I wrote the street address in my little book. It didn't take that long. And it's nothing personal. I don't even know half the people."

"So why did you slash Donald Hendrix's tire? He's as DFL as they come."

"That was an accident," she said. "He parked his Buick out front of his neighbor's house on the wrong night. How was I to know?"

"Your method is a bit slipshod," I said.

"Which is why the cops can't catch me. They look for a pattern. They can't find one. It's not IR party members. It's not always even Republicans. And now it's no longer just in central Duluth."

Kate pulled the car to rest under a huge oak tree on a residential street. She shut the motor off and we sat in silence for a few moments. A truck rumbled by on Woodland Avenue, a few blocks behind us.

"Up until the other day," she said, "there was nothing personal about this. But when I read Clarence Davies's comment in the paper . . . He called me a 'pathetic vandal.'"

"I suppose someone in your position has to expect a little negative press."

Kate turned to me. "His car is flatsville."

I laughed. "I can't believe this."

"Wait until you feel the knife slide in," she said. She smiled and reached across the car to collect the stack of notes. "Come on. And just be quiet, okay?" Kate got out of the Chevy, shutting the car door quietly behind her, and began to walk down the block. She turned and gestured for me to follow. I admit I was confused. Excited on the one hand, and fascinated that my wife had orchestrated this bizarre campaign without my slightest suspicion (not to mention the Duluth Police), and yet terrified on the other because she was a vandal, a criminal, a woman responsible for thousands of dollars' worth of ruined tires.

Kate walked a few steps back toward the car and she gave me a playful, good-natured frown—it was a look I knew well, a look she'd given me for more than thirty years, whenever she thought I was being an old grump. I almost always responded with a laugh because usually she was right, I was just being an old stick-in-the-mud. And I thought, she's going to do this with or without me—she'd already done it three dozen times—so I might as well go along for the heck of it. She kissed me on the cheek when I got out of the car, carefully pointing the knife away from us as she leaned over.

It was warmer up by the university. We were on top of the hill and back a ways from where it sloped steeply down to Lake Superior. I followed Kate down the block and around the corner and halfway down the next block. All along the way we were checking for people who might be on their porches or in their yards and who might see us, but this neighborhood was quiet. We stopped beside a brand-new-looking Ford van. Kate bent down by the right rear tire. I remained standing just behind her and she waved for me to get down beside her, which I did with some difficulty because of my leg. I was suddenly conscious of my cane—it was polished aluminum and probably quite visible in the moonlight. What if someone had seen us?

"Always at noon and at six," she said, pointing the knife to the zenith and nadir of the tire. Leaning on her left hand on the grass, she placed the tip of the knife against a spot at the top of the tire perhaps an inch from the rim. She brought the knife back an inch, then touched the tip to the tire again, marking the spot, visualizing her movements like a dart player imagining the toss, and then suddenly jabbed the knife into the tire with surprising force. She pulled the knife out and immediately the steady hiss of air filled the night, seemingly so loud I couldn't believe that the porch lights of a dozen nearby houses didn't suddenly turn on and a dozen house owners, wearing their pajamas or underwear or perhaps walking onto the porch buck naked in the summer heat, didn't step outside to see just what was going on. Kate stabbed the tire again at the bottom and then stood up. She scribbled "Fritz" at the bottom of a photocopied note, calmly walked to the front of the van and placed the note under a wiper blade, and was walking back the way we'd come before I could raise myself to a standing position, leaning heavily on my cane and cursing my aching leg.

I was having trouble walking. My leg always hurt more at night and having bent down like that behind the van had really made it sore. I hobbled along as quickly as I could. Across the street a dog started barking and a wave of fear and excitement and adrenaline crashed over me. This was for real! I hobbled along a little faster, buoyed by the sharp thrill of knowing I'd just participated in a crime.

Silly and childish, perhaps, Mr. Davies, but exhilarating.

Back at the car Kate stood with the passenger door open for me.

"Kate, you're incredible!"

"Shhh," she said. "Get in the car."

I hugged her and thanked her for sharing this with me.

The next day there was a small article on page A7 in the *Tribune* about the latest tire slashing. Oh, the secret joy of knowing, the devilish pleasure of it all! I suddenly felt closer to Kate than I had in several years. She'd let me in on one of her biggest secrets ever—we'd both told each other secrets—and for the next few weeks we lived with a kind of renewed passion that made me feel tremendously glad to be alive, to be married to Kate. We planned our next slashings. They were all to be joint endeavors from then on.

But on September the second, 1985, Kate collapsed on the floor of the kitchen while fixing lunch. Subarachnoidal hemorrhaging, undetected by the doctors. It killed her quickly.

Mr. Davies, have you ever lost a loved one? Do you know the unspeakable, insufferable sense of loss? Do you know the heart-twisting blackness that fills you when this occurs? I ask for a moment—just a moment—of sympathy in this regard, because if you can sympathize with me in the loss of my wife, you will be well on your way to understanding what drove me to commit my crime.

If you remember, then, it was in the fall of '85 that the Hillside Slasher suddenly stopped the odd campaign that had captured Duluth's attention. Eventually, the Slasher faded from memory, becoming just another odd conversation piece. A young man by the name of Jeff Watson wrote a slim book about the case; in it, he pieced together an argument suggesting that the slashings were the act of Walter Mondale's drunken, slightly deranged second cousin, Billy Theale, who also died in the fall of 1985, from liver cancer. The book sold modestly well in Duluth and I read it with some enjoyment.

But now you, Mr. Davies, you are the only living person who knows the truth, and the only reason I am telling you it is because you once asked me why. Why would a seventy-three-year-old man stick a kitchen knife in the right rear tire of your Plymouth Voyager? When you stepped out of your front door that November evening, and when I realized that I could not pull the knife back out of the tire (it requires more strength than you might think), I tried to run, but, with my bad leg, that was foolish. You tackled me onto your frozen front lawn, breaking my left leg and hip, sending me to Miller Dwan, where you leaned over my hospital bed and asked me, repeatedly and in a rather rude manner, why. I refused to answer you. I could not respond at that time. Admitting it would have resulted in my having to expose my wife's legacy—and having to pay for it, too.

So now here is your answer, Mr. Davies.

You called my wife a "pathetic vandal." She did not live to fulfill her vow of repaying you for that comment. This tire slashing was to be a kind of delayed payback. Unfortunately, I was not cut out to continue my wife's work.

I do not apologize, Mr. Davies, for slashing the tire of your Plymouth. But I do hope that you now understand why I did it. I did it for love.

Sincerely,
George Collins

Field Observations

Driving to school one morning on Highway 7 in St. Louis Park, Larry watched the car ahead of his strike and kill a raccoon. When he saw the animal tumble off into the tall grass along the shoulder, he immediately pulled over. The head had been crushed flat, but the body was intact. It seemed like a gift.

Larry's senior AP biology class had just spent two weeks dissecting cats; talk about serendipity! He drove to school with the still-warm corpse in the trunk of his '79 Volvo, quite pleased with himself. He canceled his lecture on mammalian reproduction and spent the morning classes cutting apart the raccoon. He treated it like an out-of-the-blue pop quiz. He had the students name all the major body parts. He cut open the stomach and found a very small, partially digested mouse. The students all loved it.

Dr. Kroger, the head of the science department, didn't love it. As soon as he heard about the raccoon, he called Hennepin County Animal Control, who confirmed the risk of rabies in the local raccoon population. Kroger couldn't wait until the end of school; he demanded the officials retrieve the body immediately. Later that day, Kroger called the parents of Larry's students to warn them of the risk of infection. Then it all hit the fan. The offices of the principal and the school superintendent were flooded with calls from angry parents demanding the "crazy teacher" be reprimanded, if not fired.

It didn't matter that the raccoon ultimately tested negative for rabies.

Before Larry knew it, the matter got out of hand. A reporter from the *Star-Tribune* called him at home. Larry declined to comment, but regretted that decision the next day when he saw the front-page story in the local section of the paper. Kroger had characterized him as a "rogue teacher" who "frequently put students at undue risk" in the classroom, and went on to detail several of his "stunts," including the day he'd filled his mouth with lighter fluid and sprayed it over a lit match in the lunch room.

Okay, the lighter fluid had been a mistake. But he'd apologized to Kroger and to the school principal, Emma George, for that ages ago. So much for forgive and forget. A week after the newspaper article appeared, the school district summoned him before a review board to answer some questions. Emma assured him this was mostly to appease the PTA, the media, and Kroger. She promised to go to bat for him this one time. But she warned Larry that in situations like this, where the public feels a teacher has put students at risk, there would have to be some major ass-kissing done—

her exact words—to straighten things out. And from here on out, she warned, no more stunts.

The Sunday before he was to appear before the board, a warm afternoon in late May, Larry sat at the desk in his small upstairs office. The notes for his Monday lecture on root structures in vascular plants were spread out before him like a road map. He'd tried to read the same page three times, but couldn't concentrate. He kept thinking about Kroger and the upcoming board meeting. Kroger had waited six years for a chance to slam him. Monday night would be it.

At the bottom of a page, Larry wrote NO MORE STUNTS.

Then he scratched out NO.

He stood from his desk and stretched. His office felt warm and stuffy, even with all the upstairs windows open. He took Lewis Thomas's *Lives of a Cell* from the bookshelf and scanned the dust jacket blurbs with half interest. He put the book back, then moved a paperweight from one corner of his desk to the other. He sighed and picked up his binoculars from the desk. Standing at the window, he scanned the alleyway. A cat chased something behind some garbage cans. The fat guy three houses down was mulching his roses. Again. He turned to the apartment building directly across the alley. Three flights up, left-most set of windows. In broad daylight he never saw anything inside. Just the flowers along the windowsill, dense and colorful.

He was about to give up when the back fire door of the apartment building opened and she emerged with her green reclining lawn chair and set it up in the back yard.

Her white terry cloth robe dropped from her shoulders to the grass. She wore the familiar yellow bikini. She shook out her black bob, then sat on the chair. He watched as she oiled her skin, watched her hands spread the shiny liquid over her thighs, calves, over her chest and in the small cave between her breasts.

"When was this taken?"

Startled, he turned from the window quickly. Nicole, his fiancée's daughter, stood in the doorway, looking at the photos on top of his filing cabinet. She wore scruffy blue jeans and a black Rage Against the Machine T-shirt with Che Guevara's face on it. Her blonde hair was streaked with blue and pulled back in a tight ponytail.

"Jesus, you scared me."

"I'm stealthy, huh?"

He set the binoculars lens-down on his desk. "You shouldn't do that. Sneak up on people, I mean."

"What were you looking at?"

"A squirrel." He walked over and stood beside Nicole. "Which one were you asking about?"

She pointed at a black-and-white photograph in a green frame. In it, he and some old college buddies sat side by side, cross-legged on a lawn behind a big white house. He was looking off to the right, his lower jaw protruding slightly, distending his face unhandsomely. He hadn't talked to anyone in that photograph in more than ten years.

He cleared his throat. "That was 1985, I think."

"You should've kept the long hair. You looked like a hippie."

"I'm not hip now?"

She frowned and stood back. Her loose, baggy cloth-ing gave her an androgynous look. Pam often said Nicole looked too serious, too severe for fourteen. Larry disagreed; he put it down to budding self-expression.

"You can keep the beard. Just grow your hair long. Then you'd look like Jesus."

"No thanks. I'm attracting enough unwanted atten-tion as it is."

"At least people notice you." She fiddled with the glass doorknob, rattling it back and forth. "You ever see any pictures of my mom in college?"

He shook his head.

"They're hilarious. I'll steal one for you. She was a total freak. Hair down to her butt and everything." She drew her finger along the top of the filing cabinet, col-lecting a small, gray ball of dust on her fingertip. She'd painted her nails black. "I wish she was still a hippie. She's so uptight."

"I was never really a hippie, you know. It was just a phase, something you go through in college."

Nicole shook her finger. The dustball fell slowly to the floor. She stepped on it.

"Mom says I'm going through a phase right now."

"We're always going through phases. That's life."

"Yeah, but she doesn't like this phase."

"That's because you wear Che Guevara T-shirts," he said, reaching forward and plucking her sleeve.

"You gave me this shirt."

"I did?"

Nicole frowned and punched his arm. "Idiot."

"I remember," he said, smiling and rubbing his arm as if it had really hurt. "Your last birthday."

Downstairs, Willy, his four-year-old chocolate lab, started barking.

"The probe returns," Nicole said.

They walked downstairs and met Pam and Ed, Nicole's grandfather, in the front hallway. Pam was scolding the dog for barking at her. Ed patted his forehead with a handkerchief. Plastic shopping bags were spread around their feet.

"You're supposed to return from vacation with bulging bags, not leave with them," Larry said.

"What'd you buy, the whole freaking store?"

"Nicole," Pam said, scowling. She rested her sunglasses on the top of her head. "Remember our little conversation this morning?"

"Yeah," said Nicole, thrusting her hands into her pockets.

Larry kissed Pam and hugged her. Her cheek was sticky with perspiration. "Rescue me," she whispered in his ear.

"I got something for you," Ed said to Nicole. He hadn't removed his mirrored Ray-Bans. Ed was a big man with thick arms and legs and a double chin. All that week, Larry had seen a resemblance to Alfred Hitchcock: rolypoly and a little glassy-eyed, as if he'd just had a nip from the bottle.

Ed reached down and rustled around in a plastic bag until he came up with a white cardboard box. He held it out with a pale-lipped grin.

Nicole stepped forward, chin lowered to her chest, and took the box with one hand. She spun around and quickly opened it. She pulled out a long-sleeved denim shirt with yellow-and-red flowers embroidered over the pockets.

"Eww. What's this?"

"It's a shirt," Ed said.

"Isn't it pretty?" Pam said. "Your grandfather picked it."

Larry knew then that Pam had chosen it. Ed might have offered to get something for Nicole, but there was no way he'd picked that shirt. And from Nicole's raised eyebrows, he guessed she knew this, too.

"I'll bet the busy shoppers could use a cold drink," Larry said.

"Now you're talking," Ed said, removing his sunglasses and slipping them into his shirt pocket. Beads of perspiration dotted his nose. "I didn't think it got this hot in Minneapolis."

"I'm not going to make it in the tropics," Pam said, patting the back of her head. She'd cut her hair into a short bob just a week ago, in preparation for their trip. She'd been fingering her nape ever since.

"The heat does take some getting used to," Ed said, nodding. He patted his face and scalp with the handkerchief. "I'll take a G&T, Lawrence, if you're pouring. And where are the facilities?"

"Please, just Larry." It was the third time he'd told that to Ed in a week. "The bathroom's upstairs. You can go up here," he said, pointing at the staircase, "or there's a stairway in the back hall."

"This house really does need a downstairs bathroom," Pam said.

"My fiancée needs to move in before I can remodel," Larry said, smiling. "She's the breadwinner."

"Oh, don't start on me now," she said.

"I don't want any part of this." Ed headed upstairs, muttering something under his breath.

Pam sighed. "It's been a long week."

Larry rubbed her shoulder and kissed the top of her head. "For everyone."

"Where's Nicky gone to?" she asked. "She's left her new shirt in a heap on the floor. She didn't even thank her grandfather."

Larry knelt down and refolded the shirt. The receipt was still in the box; he'd take Nicole to Dayton's later in the week and they'd exchange it for something she liked. He set the shirt in the box and pushed them off to the side of the hallway.

"I thought that was a nice shirt." She sat on the bottom step of the stairwell.

"It is a nice shirt. It's just not Nicole's style."

"She doesn't know the meaning of the word."

He sat beside her and massaged the back of her neck. The feel of her bare skin there was still new and exciting to him. He'd suggested she cut it short for her trip to the Caribbean. Surprisingly, she'd agreed. She'd had shoulder-length hair since they'd met two years ago.

"You just don't like her style."

"Not when a pair of Doc Martens cost sixty bucks. And she's got to have green, you know. Black or brown won't do." She bowed her head and moaned quietly as he rubbed. "You'll see. You'll have her for the next two weeks. The shine might rub off a little."

"That's okay. I'm thinking of it as a test drive."

He kissed the bare skin of her neck. His fingers moved down her back, massaging and caressing her shoulder blades and lower spine. He liked her petite, taut body. A runner's body. He liked wrapping his arms around her shoulders and back, holding her close to him after they'd made love, feeling her tight, damp skin as she breathed. She felt small and fragile to him then, like she needed to be protected. He'd told her that once. She'd laughed and said it sounded more like he needed someone to protect.

Pam kissed his cheek, then stood. He ran his fingers down her left leg and gently squeezed the calf. She stepped into the hall and arranged the shopping bags against one wall.

"A couple years ago she was playing with Barbies."

"And in a couple more she'll be boy crazy."

She took a tissue from her pocket and blew her nose. "Go ahead, just shoot me now." She looked around for somewhere to toss her used tissue. "Is there a wastebasket anywhere in this house?"

He held out his hand. She placed the damp tissue in it and he stuck it in his pocket. "Tell me I don't love you."

She rolled her eyes. "So, Romeo, what'd you two do while we were out shopping?"

He leaned back and rested his elbows against the steps. "Nicole listened to some music. I was trying to prep for tomorrow's classes."

"But you're too worried about the review board."

"Bingo."

"You'll be fine. Just do what Emma told you: shut up and take your medicine for once in your life."

"Maybe I don't want to cave in to Kroger like that."

She slapped her forehead. "You just never learn, do you?"

"Learning. That's the whole point. That's what I want to talk about. How to get kids to learn."

"Right, and the board wants to know why you can't stick to what's in the books."

"Because if everything you learn comes out of a book, you start thinking like Kroger, that everything has to be okayed before you can study it. I want these kids to think for themselves. The Latin root—"

"—I know, I know, the Latin root of educate is *educere*, which means to draw out, not to cram in. I've heard this lecture." She waved a hand in the air as if brushing away a fly. "You're just a little too much sometimes, you know that?"

She rearranged a small brass elephant in the center of the table near the door. Both elephant and table had been gifts from her last Christmas. Her first attempt at decorating his Spartan house. He knew that when she and Nicole moved in next August, after the wedding, everything would change. The sooner the better, he thought.

"This isn't a pedagogical debate," she said. "It's politics. These people can fire you. What you need right now is spin control, not a bully pulpit."

"You think what I did was wrong."

"No, I know you. You always try to do the right thing."

"Not always," he said. He stood and walked to her and wrapped his arms around her waist. "We need to talk when you get back," he murmured. "I want you to move in before August."

"I need to survive this trip, first," she said, drawing a fingertip down the front of his shirt. "But I'll tell you this much: I'm not moving in with an unemployed schoolteacher."

"What ever happened to 'love conquers all?'"

"That's the kind of thinking that got me into my first marriage," she said, "the one where what I thought was stability turned out to be rigidity. And all those crazy and exciting personality traits turned out to be capital-D dysfunctional."

He moved a hand up and down her back. "I'm not like that."

"No, I don't believe you are." She kissed him. "Just promise me you'll do what Emma told you to do, okay?"

"Mmm. I promise to maybe do what I'm told. Some of the time."

"And you think you're going to make a great stepfather, huh?" She turned away from him and checked her hair in the small mirror by the front door. "Why on earth did you tell me to get this bob? Why did I listen to you?"

Larry had bought the binoculars for field observations. At least once every school year he took a group of students to Theodore Wirth Park, or Fort Snelling, and they spent an afternoon watching and cataloguing as many birds as possible. Then there were the prairie dogs and the bison out at the zoo. He'd seen bear and moose in the BWCA. Binoculars were simply essential for a working biologist. For years, they'd hung in a leather case on an old hat rack in his office. He never thought to use them for anything other than watching nature.

Late one summer evening, near sunset, he sat in his office at home watching an oriole. The bird suddenly flew away, and as he followed it the binoculars fell on the apartment building across the alley, where he saw a woman, topless, come to her window and water her plants. She was shapely, with dark, short hair. He sat in his chair, feet on the windowsill, and watched her for the minute or two it took to water her plants. Then she disappeared.

He thought little of it. It had been an accident, the kind of once-in-a-blue-moon thing you see when you live in a city, pressed up close to people.

But then a couple of days later he saw the same woman sunbathing in the back yard of the apartment building. He knew he shouldn't, but he grabbed the binocs and watched her. Really watched her. He watched her abdomen rise and fall as she breathed. He studied her breasts, her cheeks, the curves of her thighs.

He didn't watch her every day. But he watched often enough that he began to get a sense of her routine. Pretty soon, he'd invented a life for her, which he knew to be a fiction. Yet it seemed compelling. There were facts and deductions. She lived alone. Worked until about eight at night. She rarely lowered the blinds in her apartment, and she liked to walk around topless.

He really didn't want to know any more than that. He wanted gaps in the story. Watching her was like viewing a silent film: you pieced it together from disparate fragments and images. And the act was easier for him to excuse when he reminded himself that he really didn't know the woman, didn't know if she were a nurse or an aerobics instructor, a schoolteacher or a mechanic. It was precisely this not-knowing that allowed him to continue watching. If he even knew so much as her name, he told himself, he would have to stop. There were boundaries. And yet it was the act of walking that line—or the knowledge that he had stepped over the line, and that he was capable of doing so again and again—that gave him a secret thrill.

You'd never want someone to know this about you. They'd never think it of you. You didn't like to think it of yourself.

Ed stood in the back yard with one foot up on a lawn chair, his G&T in one hand and the other hand waving around in the air, dangerously close to the plates and bowls lining the edge of the lawn table.

"The problem is simple," he said. "When Maurice Bishop took over, him and his People's Revolutionary so-called Government, they had no right to seize the foreigners' land. I own that land. Ten acres of prime beachfront property in St. David's parish. I have the deed, a legal document stamped and signed by Her Majesty's government. And now that saner heads are prevailing down there, I aim to get it back." He lifted his drink in a toast. "With a little help from my daughter, the lawyer," he added.

"Watch the onions," said Larry. He shuffled the nearly finished burgers around on the Weber, sweating in the humid afternoon heat.

Pam sat at the table, under the shade of the parasol, sipping her G&T. Nicole had been throwing a ball for Willy in the far corner of the back lawn, but had disappeared somewhere.

"You see, I knew Maurice Bishop. I had lunch with him several times, in fact, when he was a lawyer. Politics ruined him. He had these crazy plans. Take all the foreigners' land. Seize their assets. Then give them back to 'the people.'"

"Well, they were communists," said Larry. "Redistribution of wealth. It's textbook Marxism."

"Totally bunk." Ed sipped his drink.

"What's so bunk about it?"

Ed looked straight at Larry for a long moment.

Larry flashed a quick grin. "Just for the sake of argument."

"You're the schoolteacher. It's A-B-C as far as I'm concerned. For a little country like Grenada to make it, they need foreign investment. Capital. They need every cent they can get."

"Granted. So what difference does it make if the money comes from Washington or Moscow?"

Ed laughed and turned to Pam. "Your fiancé's got a strange sense of humor, Pammy."

"Tell me something I don't know. Hey, is this Beefeater?"

"Gordon's," Larry said. "On sale. Just go on with your story, Ed, and I promise not to butt in. You were just getting to the American invasion. You were in favor of it, I assume."

Ed set the empty glass on the table. "'Intervention' is the preferred word."

Larry wiped his brow with the back of his hand. "There's a difference?"

"You bet your tookus. It was an intervention, and a much-needed intervention at that. Reagan did the right thing. That's what makes this country great. We've got guts. We can strike when necessary, like in Grenada. Or Iraq. Survival of the fittest, right Professor?" He slapped Larry's shoulder.

"Evolution isn't about conflict. It's about adaptability."

"Frame it any way you like."

Larry put his spatula down and picked up the plate with the sliced cheddar. Beads of grease had formed on the cheese in the hot sun.

"I think I prefer Beefeater," Pam said.

"You like cheese on your burger, Ed?"

"Two slices."

Nicole appeared suddenly from around the corner of the house. Dirt stained her knees, as if she'd been digging. She ran up behind her mother's chair.

"Did anyone miss me?"

"Miss who," said Pam.

Nicole stuck out her tongue.

"I did," Larry said. "Where on earth have you been?"

Nicole produced a handful of dandelions from behind her back. She handed one each to Ed, Pam, and Larry.

"Did you know that every dandelion is a clone? They don't have to have sex to reproduce, right, Larry?"

Pam looked at him, pulling her sunglasses down her nose an inch and lifting her eyebrows. "Oh, do tell, Professor."

Larry smiled. "She's right. Dandelions reproduce asexually. Barring genetic mutation, all offspring are identical."

"Interesting," Pam said, pushing her sunglasses back up. "I can't wait to hear what she'll be talking about when I get back."

"I like biology," said Nicole. "Larry makes it fun."

"Gimme five," Larry said, holding out his palm. Nicole slapped it.

Ed tossed his ice cubes out onto the lawn. "I'm getting another splash. Anyone need a filler-upper?"

Pam and Larry shook their heads.

"Back in a few," Ed said, trundling off for the patio door.

A moment later, Nicole said, "I want a Coke," and ran inside.

Pam straightened herself in the lawn chair. "You know, you ought to take it easy on my father."

"What, that Grenada stuff? I was just goofing around," he said, placing the cheese slices on the burgers. He put two on Ed's burger.

"I know what you're doing. I'm just telling you. Dad has a short temper sometimes, especially after he's had a couple drinks."

"A couple? That's his fourth. At least."

"I told you, he drinks," she said, sharply.

He nodded. She'd been testy all week. He'd put it down to Ed's visit, and the pressure she felt to accompany him to Grenada to look after his affairs. It seemed the best thing he could offer her at that moment was silence—a thought which simultaneously irritated and intrigued him.

The patio door slid open violently, rocking against the end of its track. Nicole, her face contorted with crying, ran onto the deck. "I hate you!" she screamed, then ran around the corner of the house.

Ed's deep voice boomed from the kitchen. "Nicole!"

"Oh, shit," Pam said. "Shit shit shit."

"I'll go after Nicky," Larry said, picking the burgers off the grill. "You go see about your old man."

He found Nicole sitting on a bench in the small city park a few blocks from his house. He felt this was where she'd go; they'd come many times to shoot baskets or let Willy chase tennis balls. He sat beside her on the bench facing the basketball courts. Ten women ran up and down the court, shouting to each other to make passes, their sneakers squeaking on the cement. He liked watching them in their tank tops and sports bras, sweating so intensely in the heat.

Nicole sat with her legs folded under her, an index finger inches from her nose. On her fingertip was a bright orange ladybug.

"Tell me something about ladybugs."

A tall, leggy woman who looked a little like Whoopi Goldberg crashed up against the fence, reaching for an out-of-bounds ball.

"Well, first off, they're beetles, not bugs. Second, not all ladybugs are ladies."

She maneuvered her hand as the ladybug crawled down her finger. It opened its orange-and-black shell, extending its wings.

"They're so weird looking. How do they . . . you know?"

"Same as us. The male passes sperm into the female. What's different is, she lays her eggs in waterproof shells and then she's done. The eggs develop on their own."

Nicole looked up from her hand. "No parents?"

He shook his head.

"Cool." They ladybug flew from her fingertip. "Bye."

Whoopi faked somebody at the top of the key, took a step back, and drained a jumper.

"You ready to come back to the house?"

She took a strand of hair and drew it into her mouth. "I'm just in everyone's way."

"You're not in my way."

"You're different," she said. "You're cool. You're not like them. You're more like . . ."

"A kid?"

"No, you're not a kid. You're just . . . I don't know. What are you, anyway?"

"I get in people's way." He flicked a mosquito from his knee. "Are you going to come and be my cheerleader at this board meeting tomorrow night? I could use one."

"The thing about the raccoon?"

He nodded.

"I don't have to talk to anyone, do I?"

"No, I'll be doing all the talking. Or maybe I'll just be listening. I haven't made up my mind."

"I think I like you because you're an adult but you still get in trouble."

He laughed. "Better not tell your mom that. She won't let you stay with me."

Nicole brushed her hair back behind an ear. "Is everything going to be the same after you two shack up?"

"Probably not."

She folded her arms across her chest. "Then don't do it."

He thought then that he ought to say something, to have some comforting words or a pithy piece of advice. Even a bad joke. But somehow his silence seemed most appropriate. They sat quietly for several minutes, until the basketball players took a break. Larry and Nicole stood up to leave. A short, tanned woman walked to the chain-link fence, a few feet from them, and picked up a water bottle and drank. She took off a hair band and shook out her thick, black bob. Larry stopped dead in his tracks.

"Come on, Larry," shouted Nicole, sprinting off. "Race you!"

The woman turned at the sound of Nicole's voice and met his gaze. She had haunting, pale gray eyes. Looking straight into them, he felt miles away.

She looked off at Nicole, then back to him. Her brow furrowed.

"You want something, Larry?" Her voice was gravelly and hoarse.

His face burned. "I'm sorry," he said, turning and walking after Nicole, who was halfway across the softball diamond. He buried his hands in his trouser pockets, absently digging after loose change.

Pam sat on the front steps of the house, drinking a cup of coffee. She smiled as Larry and Nicole approached, and patted the spot beside her for Nicole to sit down. She did so.

"I'm taking him back to my place," Pam said. "He's had too much to drink. I'm sorry, Larry. My father hasn't exactly shown you his best side this week."

He shrugged his shoulders. The front yard was blanketed in shadows and felt cooler. A few houses down some kids were playing whiffle ball in the street, the plastic ball bouncing off car hoods.

"Nicole deserves the apology, not me."

"I'm sorry, honey," Pam said, hugging Nicole. She looked up at Larry. Her eyes were bloodshot. She'd been crying.

A loud clatter came from inside the house, like a tray of silverware falling to the floor.

Pam frowned. "I tried to have a talk with him. It didn't go well. He's in the living room. Could you tell him that we'll be leaving in a few minutes? I want to talk to Nicky."

"Sure," Larry said, touching Nicole's shoulder as he passed.

He walked back to the kitchen. Ed was bent over the sink, clearing his throat. The dirty dishes had been stacked messily to one side. On the counter, the gin was uncapped. The tonic bottle was empty.

Ed ran the tap, rinsed his hands and face, then shut off the tap and turned around. There were damp stains around his belly, as if he'd dried his hands on his own shirt. He fixed a glassy, sullen stare on Larry.

Larry tossed him a kitchen towel. "You feeling okay?"

Ed dried his face and arms, then threw the balled-up towel over by the coffeemaker. He cupped a big, meaty hand around the gin bottle.

"Where's my glass?"

Larry leaned a hip against the counter. "Pam says you guys are heading out in a few."

Ed pushed the bottle away and opened a cabinet. "Where's my glass? I need one for the road."

Larry screwed the cap back on the gin and set the bottle against the wall. "Party's over."

Ed closed the cabinet and turned to Larry. "You're a wise guy, huh? Think you know something."

Larry folded his arms across his chest. Willy stood at the patio door, whining, his pink tongue throbbing against the screen.

Ed took a step toward Larry, narrowing his eyes. "To you everything is a big joke."

"I wish," Larry said, pushing himself off the counter and walking around Ed.

"Get me a glass. Where are you going?"

"I'm letting my dog in."

Larry slid open the screen door for Willy. The dog lapped at his water bowl, then trotted off down the hall. Larry closed and latched the screen door. He saw the top two floors of her apartment building looming over his small garage. She knew his name. That fact seemed hard, indigestible. The more he thought of it, the less he understood.

He heard Pam's and Nicole's voices on the front porch, talking in a soft murmur.

He turned and walked back into the kitchen. Ed was gone. So was the gin.

He checked the living room. Then the laundry room. Ed wasn't downstairs. He climbed the back staircase slowly. The bathroom door was closed and locked.

"Ed," he said.

The tap ran, then stopped. Then the sound of something—a bottle cap—falling to the tile floor.

"Ed, listen. You can have the damn bottle. Take it with you, if you want."

The phone rang. He walked down the hall and into his office. It was Emma George. She'd been thinking about the review board on Monday and wanted to touch base.

"How're you feeling?" she asked.

"You really want to know?"

"Probably not. Listen, I just got off the phone with the commissioner about tomorrow night. A contrite apology will do. Of course, they have to let Kroger have his say, so be ready for that."

He picked up his binoculars and walked to the window. He scanned the back yard of the apartment building. The lawn chair was there, but empty.

"Do I get a say?"

"You mean, other than, 'I'm really sorry?'"

"Yeah. I mean, Kroger's going to go off in front of all those people, in front of the parents. And the kids. Shouldn't I explain my side of it?"

"I don't know," she said. "What are you driving at?"

"Accountability. I want these parents to know who I am. You have to take responsibility for what you do, don't you think?"

"Apologizing is a form of taking responsibility."

He lifted the binoculars to the third floor, left-most apartment. The blinds were down. He was glad for that.

"True," he said. "But it doesn't explain the question of why."

Emma sighed loudly. "Damn it, I thought we saw eye-to-eye on this. You want to talk about taking responsibility? I just brown-nosed the commissioner for you. We reached an *understanding*. Do you know what I'm really saying here?"

"They're letting women into the Old Boys Club?"

There was a long pause. He trained his gaze on the empty lawn chair. Took a good, long look. It seemed the best way to leave things.

"Okay, do it your way. The board can't fire you for this, not this first time. But they could suspend you. Or write a nasty complaint for your file, which Kroger would only be too happy to sign. If another incident or two came up later, you could be terminated."

When he didn't respond, she said, "We're talking about your career here, Larry. You really ought to play it by the book tomorrow night."

"I know, Emma."

"Well then?"

"Thanks for everything you did for me," he said. And he hung up.

Ed cleared his throat in the doorway. "In Grenada, they rub red pepper in the eyes of a Peeping Tom."

Larry lowered the binoculars and turned from the window.

"I was watching a bird."

"Sure you were." Ed laughed. "You know, Pammy told me about you."

"She did," he said, as flatly as he could manage. Why hadn't she *said* something? He put the binoculars back in their leather case and snapped shut the lid. Everybody knew his name.

"She said you're passionate about what you do, but pig-headed as hell. We're a lot alike in that regard." He stepped into the office and looked at Larry's framed degree on the wall, cradling a glass against his chest. It was the small glass Larry kept his toothbrush in, from the bathroom.

"You want to know why I'm really going back to Grenada?"

Larry dropped into his office chair. "No."

"It has nothing to do with the land. I wrote that off years ago." He turned to Larry. He licked his lips and squinted his eyes a little, as if he were having difficulty focusing.

"I've got a dozen plots of land that size back in California," he said, shrugging his shoulders. Gin slopped over the rim of the glass, darkening the breast of his shirt. "And enough in the bank to retire on three times. It's the principle of the thing. I liked what you said about accountability on the phone just now. I agree with that."

Larry lifted his eyebrows.

"I was spying on you." He tapped Larry's shin with his loafer. "Everybody does it."

Larry frowned.

Pam's voice echoed from downstairs. "Dad? Larry? Are you guys coming?"

"Give us a minute," Ed boomed. He stepped forward and leaned over to look out the window. He whistled. "At least you've got taste."

Larry didn't look.

"It's time for you to go, Ed."

Ed stepped away from the window. He drained his gin in several large gulps, then set the wet glass on top of Larry's lecture notes for Monday, ink blearing as the alcohol soaked into the paper.

Ed wiped the back of his hand across his mouth. "You know, on second thought, I'm not sure I like you."

A sharp word came to Larry's tongue, but he swallowed it. There had to be some measure of grace possible, even now. He stood and shrugged his shoulders. "Join the club, I guess."

He left the office and walked down the staircase to the front entryway. A bright patch of late afternoon sun illuminated part of a wall and the hardwood floor, filling the hall with a soft glow. Pam and Nicole both stood with noses pressed against the screen door, their somber faces speaking only of the immediacy of departure.

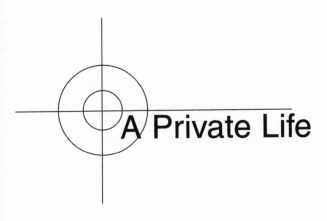

A Private Life

The garden was overdue for a weeding. Thistles surrounded the tomato plants. A blanket of thin-stemmed grass threatened to choke the peppers. Women passing Jo's narrow streetside garden had taken to mentioning it. "You better tend to dat," they'd say, nodding toward the cramped plot, "or weeds go choke you vegetable quite out." Sometimes the advice was delivered with a smile, woven in amidst some bit of chatter about the weather. Other times it was a stern command, delivered with a frown and a wag of the finger. Regardless, Jo smiled and acted as if she hadn't realized weeds could harm a garden, promising to see to it right away. The old women shuffled off shaking their heads, laughing at the white woman who obviously didn't know the first thing.

That morning, Jo knelt on a piece of folded cardboard. She plucked weeds haphazardly, without any thought to a plan, tossing them—beautiful in their own right, she thought, thin roots defiantly clutching damp earth—in a pile to one side. For tough weeds, she used a kitchen fork long ago sacrificed for the cause, its stem bent and folded like a sine wave. The ground teemed with life. Out of each tiny hole scurried beetles, worms, millipedes. She enjoyed the rhythm of digging, plucking, tossing, and the rich, mulchy smell of the earth. The sun was warm on her neck and shoulders.

To her right, Main Street bustled with Saturday morning traffic and pedestrians. Buses and taxis tooted their horns in greeting. People called to one another on the street. A man pushing a wheelbarrow heaped with papaya stopped to lift his straw hat and bid her a good morning. She sat back on her feet and returned the gesture. It was when she stood to accept the man's offer of a plump, ripe melon that she noticed the thin boy standing near her gate, one bare foot resting atop the other, hands buried in the pockets of his shorts. He wore a stained, dusty T-shirt and had thick, burrish hair in need of a trim.

"Hello there," Jo said.

A wide smile crossed the boy's face. He turned his gaze to the street.

"What are you doing today?" she asked. When he did not respond, she added, "Or do you just like to watch the funny white lady work in her garden?"

The boy brought a hand to his mouth to cover the toothy grin.

It was part of being white and living on a small Caribbean island. Everything she did seemed noteworthy to someone, usually children. Once, a little girl had followed her around Bullen's grocery, unabashedly staring as Jo filled her basket with a bag of rice, a few tins of soup, a jar of pepper sauce. Ordinary things. And then one morning at home, after only a couple weeks on island, she'd taken her easel and watercolors out to the sandy front yard of her beachside cottage to paint the colorful sloops anchored in Hillsborough Bay. She'd looked up from her work to find a half dozen small children lining her fence, their wide-eyed gazes fixed on her. When she'd greeted them, they'd burst out giggling and scampered off, only to return a few minutes later. The process repeated itself several times until Jo began to resent the attention and took her things inside.

In her six months on Carriacou, this benign voyeurism had become less frequent. It helped that, as a nurse, she traveled all over the small island, visiting the village health clinics. People now recognized her, often greeted her by name. But while the stares were less unsettling, she'd never wholly made peace with the disquieting feeling of being on display. Some days it seemed as if people were watching every little thing she did, no matter how banal or trivial. And so it did not surprise her to find this ragged boy standing just out of view, watching her weed her garden with a kitchen fork.

She asked his name, and he told her: Cap.

"I've got a lot of weeds, don't I, Cap?" She guessed his age to be twelve.

He stepped forward and craned his neck to see. He nodded. "You must stake dem tomato plant better," he said, judiciously. "When dey ripe and you have big fruit, dey go bend down. Dem little stick you use ehn strong enough."

"Where could I get better stakes?"

Cap nodded down the street. "Dollar Mahn sell good ones at he shop." He lowered his gaze to the sidewalk, pushing at a bottle cap with his toe. "Or ah could cut you some from a tree."

Jo smiled. "How much would they cost at Dollar Man's store?"

"I ehn know. Two dollars."

"I'll tell you what. You go ahead and cut me some stakes from a tree branch and I'll pay you the two dollars I would have spent at the shop. How does that sound?"

Cap looked up and smiled broadly. "Ah going to come right back, Miss."

It was when he turned to amble off that she saw how one leg was much shorter and thinner than the other. He walked with an awkward limp that made his shoulders bounce.

The boy returned a half hour later with several stout, straight boughs much sturdier than the thin doweling Jo had used to support her young plants. Cap staked and tied her tomatoes and also gave her tips on the peppers, suggesting she mix spent tea leaves into the soil at their base.

"You know a lot about gardening," she said, later, after she'd paid him and poured him a glass of lemonade. They sat in white plastic lawn chairs under the shade of her narrow front porch, looking out onto the bright blue water of Hillsborough Bay.

"Mummy have big, big garden," he said. "She have a table in de market. Is always Cap dat help tend she garden. With me leg so, ah cyan work de sloop to help me Poopa fish."

"How did your leg get that way?"

He patted the atrophied limb. "Mummy say ah catch a fever when ah just a little baby. After dat, me leg ehn grow right. Ah cyan remember. It always been so."

"You ever have a doctor look at it?"

He shook his head.

"You should. Come by the Hillsborough Clinic next Tuesday when Dr. Singh visits. Let him take a look at it."

"Dat you Indian friend?"

Jo straightened in her chair. "Dr. Singh? We're friendly, yes. Of course."

"You two move real easy together," Cap said, smiling. "Mummy say it nice to see de white lady find a friend."

Jo drew in her lower lip. "Is that right?"

"It a good ting, eh? Womahn need a mahn to protect she here. Keep she safe safe," Cap said, turning his cup around in his hand. "Well, ah making a move." He finished his lemonade, thanked her, then promised to visit again soon to help with the garden. Jo waved good-bye from her seat.

She thought of Rami Singh. It was he who insisted they keep a polite distance in public. He who insisted that they make love only in his flat, with the doors locked and the shades down. He claimed his position demanded discretion. For a time, she hadn't minded. It was a game, a covert operation, a shared secret. And the payoff was there: as a lover, he was athletic, experienced, patient. He hungered for her, luring her to his flat directly after work, undressing her piece by piece as he knelt before her in his living room, reverently tasting every inch of her skin with his mouth. His passion for her was humbling.

But the gig was up. Nothing she'd done in her six months on the island had garnered nearly as much attention as her affair with Rami Singh. People went out of their way, it seemed, to make note of it. It was no mystery why. People saw them together. People talk, and talk gets around. It only gets you down if pretending the talk isn't true seems wholly asinine.

She met Rami at noon in the narrow brick plaza out front of the Grentel offices. It took her a second to pick him out; dressed in acid-washed blue jeans rolled to his shins and a loose dress shirt, he blended right in with the young men loitering about the plaza's pay phones, as if expecting them to ring. To Jo, he nodded curtly; he waved farewell to the men. One of them hissed at her, a come-on. She ignored it.

Rami wore an old pair of yellow flip-flops, which clacked as they made their way down the street. A stained white croker sack slung over his shoulder swayed gently to the rhythm of his gait. Jo smelled the coconut suntan oil she'd doused herself with before leaving.

"You look very colonial today."

"Colonial?" she said. "Excuse me?"

"White pants. White shirt. Straw hat." He took a cigarette from his shirt pocket and lit it as they walked. "If some old fruit picker were to see us today, walking the groves of the plantation, he might have a heart attack, thinking he's seeing the ghost of his former oppressor."

His voice sounded so sharp; it made her pause. Then he burst out laughing, that familiar, high roll of chuckles. He turned and winked.

"You're such a bullshitter," she said, slapping his upper arm.

"A physician's prerequisite, no?"

He led her across the secondary school's cricket pitch, which in the rainy season doubled as a pasture. Half a dozen sheep and two cows were staked out on thick rope. The smell of fresh manure rose around her.

"You know, Tom Waring still owns this plantation," she said. "I asked a lady in the market about it. He's been known to chase people off with a cutlass."

Rami waved a hand as if brushing off a fly. "Waring himself won't be doing anything of the sort today. He's been in a hospital bed in Grenada for the past two weeks. Broken hip, the old fool."

"Well, won't there be a caretaker or something?"

He stopped and reached a hand around her back, giving her shoulder a gentle squeeze. They stood beside a cement-lined sluice that was full of scrub, empty plastic bags, and soda bottles whose labels had long ago been bleached white in the tropical sun. The sluice ran directly onto Hillsborough Beach. After a big rain, the beach filled with garbage not, as she'd once thought, washed ashore from other islands or careless yachties, but from Carriacou's interior.

"Here is where my position as the island's physician pays off," he said, in a low tone. "The caretaker is one Septimus Greenleaf." He smiled knowingly.

She lifted her eyebrows. "Who?"

"Boil on his left shoulder? We lacerated it together last Tuesday."

"Oh, yes," she said, frowning. It had been a messy affair.

"Today we operate with his blessings," he said, hopping forward over the sluice, then turning and extending a hand to her. She declined it, hopping across easily on her own.

"Well, that's good to hear. Do me a favor and don't get me chopped with a cutlass."

He laughed. She followed him across a dirt road and then along a narrow goat track through a bramble-ridden pasture. It was mid-November, the height of the rainy season. The sweet-smelling new grass stood tall and thick around them. The tips of Jo's leather sneakers darkened with moisture. For a few minutes, walking through a thick copse of breadfruit and mango trees, she felt disoriented. The sensation pleased her. On a thirteen-square-mile island, you don't feel lost very often.

Twenty minutes later, they were climbing a steep hillside under the heavy shade of low-hanging tree limbs. Damp fern crowded the path. Jo slipped on a patch of wet leaves, falling to one knee and staining her white trousers.

"Where is this lime grove?"

"We're not going to the main plantation in Prospect Hall," Rami said. "Septimus told me of a lesser-known spot in Beausejour, though it is a bit of a hike."

"I didn't know I was going on an expedition. I'd have worn my boots."

"Yes, the colonist likes to be prepared."

Laughing, she threw a handful of leaves at him. He smirked and continued walking. They came over a rise and stepped into a narrow grove divided into neat rows of lime, grapefruit, and orange trees.

"This is the sole remaining plot from the original Waring plantation," he said, "dating back to sixteen-something. They long ago converted most of this hillside to mahogany, and their other land exclusively to limes and cotton. Whatever sold best at the time. But, according to Septimus, who is something of a historian, the fruit trees on this plot are among the oldest Waring owns. He kept this tiny little grove as a memento of sorts. And, I need not add, as a splendid source of fresh fruit."

He walked to a nearby tree and, reaching up on his tiptoes, plucked a plump yellow grapefruit. He took a knife from his jeans pocket and quickly quartered it in his palm. He handed her a slice. It was beautiful, pink and swollen with juice. She bit into it.

"Delicious," she said, puckering her lips.

"Yes," he said, biting a slice slowly. "We shall fill our bags with as much as we can carry. With, I repeat, the full blessings of Mr. Septimus Greenleaf."

When they'd finished eating the grapefruit, Rami took the croker sack from his shoulder and began to fill it with fruit, zig-zagging between the three varieties of trees. As he picked, he sang a children's counting song in a high, silly voice that made her laugh. She followed him, plucking from low-hanging branches. The path was littered with wasted fruit, rotting in the grass. He tossed oranges into her canvas grocery sack from several feet off, calling himself the West Indian Michael

Jordan. They laughed when he hit a shot; they laughed when he missed. He threw a lime high up in the air and then ran to catch it in his croker sack; improbably, he did. They laughed. When he tugged forcefully on a recalcitrant grapefruit and another, smaller grapefruit fell onto his head, they laughed again.

Their bags were bulging by the time they'd made it three-quarters of the way through the grove. Setting his sack down at the base of a tree, he told her to leave her bag. She followed him between two rows of lime trees, up the gently sloped hillside to a wide, rectangular patch of grass. He led her to its uppermost edge, at the foot of a stout mahogany tree, and then bid her turn around.

Below was the town of Hillsborough, with its tight grid of narrow streets and densely clustered buildings. Beyond that, a thin lip of white sand and then the bright blue bay, giving out onto the Caribbean. The view was nowhere near as breathtaking or picturesque as the one from the front lawn of Princess Royal Hospital, high atop the hills of Belair. But she was mesmerized nonetheless; this perspective foregrounded the secondary school and the power plant—places she normally thought of as being behind Main Street. She noted, with pleasure, that her tiny blue cottage was obscured by the double-storied guest house across the street.

"Is Guyana as lovely as this?" she asked.

"Parts of it, naturally," he said. "If you want my honest opinion, Carriacou is too dry and barren. There are some beaches along the Guyanese coast so beautiful it would make you weep. But our inland rain forests are the real treasure."

She reached an arm around his waist and pulled herself close. "Take me there."

He ran a hand slowly up and down her back, then stepped away. "Of course, I am from Georgetown, the capital. And it is a large city much like any other in the Caribbean. Crowded, smelly, and hot. You would not like it." He lingered a few feet from her for a moment, then walked down the hillside and disappeared into the grove.

She stood at the crest of the clearing, letting the cool November breeze dry her brow. They'd flirted almost from the day he'd arrived six weeks before. Everyone at PR had noticed; how could it be avoided, with a staff of four? She'd taken their ribbing in stride. Ditto for the rumors: he'd lost his medical license in Guyana; he'd gotten a nurse pregnant; he was fleeing a stifling marriage.

Still, there *was* an awful lot she didn't know. Getting personal information out of him was like picking a bank safe. He planned to return to Guyana for two weeks during the December holidays, but to whom? His six-month contract on Carriacou expired at the end of March. There was no chance of renewal. Dr. Hutchison, the island's permanent resident physician, would be back from holiday. She had no future with Rami.

That was precisely what had tempted her, initially. That, and his Cambridge accent. And his penchant for silk ascots, which she found oddly irresistible. He was handsome, no two ways about it: thin, muscular, and toned, with high cheekbones and warm, brown eyes. His skin gave off the luster of cinnamon butter, and tasted as sweet. Yes, for a time, she'd liked everything about him.

A cloud shadow crossed the bay, temporarily darkening the water's vivid, vibrant blue.

Rami sat in the mahogany-frame chair, legs crossed at the knees. His empty Tom Collins glass rested on the dark, glossy varnish of the chair's arm. The evening sun threw a pattern of distended, yellow-red rectangles across the tiled floor. Jo lay stretched out on the full-length couch in her underwear and a T-shirt.

"I don't think I can leave this couch," she said.

He ran his fingers across his mouth and smiled. "I don't want you to leave that couch."

"You think I'm joking."

The half-empty pitcher of rum and fresh fruit juice stood sweating on the floor between them.

"I could sponge you down in a cool shower," he said. "Stay the night. You know my king-sized bed is much more comfortable than your little cot."

"This *couch* is more comfortable than my cot," she said, propping herself up on her elbows. Her clothes lay in a heap at her feet. Her skin felt sticky with the day's perspiration. She sat upright and swung her feet around to the floor.

"I'm going to have one more glass of this rum punch, and then I'm heading home. I'm beat." She really didn't need another drink; he'd mixed them strong. She already felt lightheaded and sleepy.

He leaned forward and refilled her glass.

"Without any cuddles?"

"You don't want to cuddle with me now," she said, tartly. "I'm sweaty and smelly."

He handed her the full glass. "Oh, but I like that. There's something very sexy about a woman like you, all dirty and hot."

"A saucy white colonist?" she said, sipping the rum punch. "You'd be sleeping with the enemy."

He laughed. "I suppose someone must."

"You speak of it as a duty."

"On the contrary, it is an honor and a privilege."

"Spare me," she said, holding up a hand. She reached for her trousers. They were damp and heavy. As she stood and pulled them up to her waist, she felt suddenly conscious of him watching her.

He stood from his chair. "Stay," he said, stepping forward and lifting a hand to her cheek. He brushed a strand of hair back behind her ear.

He embraced her and she let him. It was tempting to give in to him. Again. Him and his world, his way of seeing things. His definitions. His rules.

"No," she said, placing a hand against his warm chest and pushing herself back slightly. "Not now. Not tonight."

"I need you," he whispered. His arms were still wrapped around her waist. She lowered her forehead to his shoulder. He smelled of cologne and body sweat— not a mix that worked. They swayed together for several minutes, dancing silently. He slipped a hand underneath her shirt and began lightly caressing her back.

"I know you're married," she whispered, half hoping he wouldn't hear.

He stiffened slightly, but then moved closer, nuzzling her head, murmuring, "This is a love affair, my dear. No one ever said anything about forever."

She gently pushed him away.

"No," she said.

"I see." He removed his arms and stepped back. With a deep sigh, he turned in a half circle and slapped his hands against his thighs. He lit a cigarette and drew on it thoughtfully. "Who told you I was married?"

"Are you?"

"Don't you know?" he said, sharply. "Never mind. You need not reveal your sources. On Carriacou people gossip. It is what passes for a good time around here."

She frowned. She'd wanted him to deny it, to laugh it off, to prove her wrong. She reached for her shoes and socks.

"I'm sorry," he said, stepping forward and placing a warm hand on her forearm. She lifted her eyes to him, her jaw set tight. He let go.

"You fancy me a liar now. Duplicitous." He chuckled. "Does it really bother you?"

"Yes. I don't know." She lifted her canvas sack, bulging with fruit. "Maybe you're just devious. I still like you, if that means anything."

"Oh, it does," he sneered, leaning over to pick up his cigarettes from the coffee table. "We can be friends, as you Americans are fond of saying."

Jo laughed, despite herself. She couldn't help it. She opened the front door. A scrap of white paper, blown this way and that by the wind, flipped and twirled across the street below.

"You know, if you were just open with me . . ."

"What," he said. "What then?"

She turned. He sat on the edge of the couch, studying the cigarette box in his hands.

She let herself out the door, closing it behind her with a soft click.

Jo walked slowly along Main Street. She passed a small rum shop, a board shack with a bare bulb hanging inside it, some stools and a bar. AM radio murmured behind the voices of men, shouting and laughing as they slapped dominoes onto a table. At the corner of Patterson and Main, in Market Square, a three-legged dog paused from lapping gutter water to follow her for a few feet, yapping needlessly. She turned and reached a hand down to the sidewalk, pretending to pick up a stone. The dog immediately fled.

She heard laughter, and turned to meet the gaze of two officers in their shirtsleeves, loitering along the second-story balcony of the police station.

"Eh, white womahn," one called. "You looking good and strong."

The other man laughed and slapped his friend on the shoulder.

She ignored them. This is what passed for protection on Carriacou.

"Eh eh? Is how you pass me straight? Come here, baby."

She clutched her bag tightly to her chest and walked faster. She wanted only a long, warm shower and to fall into bed, alone, and sleep. She'd turn her phone off, draw the curtains, and hole up for a while. She let herself in the iron gate facing Main Street. As she walked along the side of the house, she noticed the porch light was off. She thought perhaps it had burned out. She was scrupulous about leaving it on whenever she left her house, even if she knew she'd be back early. She never wanted to come home to a darkened porch.

Stepping up onto the narrow concrete slab before her front door, her feet crunched on something light and fine. She thought it might be sand, or gravel. It was broken glass. Above her, the porch light had been knocked clean out. A tangled bit of thin wire dangled from the socket. She set the bag of fruit down, dug into her pocket for the house key, and slid it into the kitchen door handle. The lock turned with no resistance. She paused. Then she saw that someone had tapped out the lowest, left-hand pane of glass, near the door handle.

For a long moment, she did not, could not move. She gripped the handle fiercely. She heard nothing from within. Only the soft roll of waves on the beach behind her and a dog barking somewhere far off down the street. Then, in the yard, just a few feet behind her, a rustle of palm leaves and the deadened sound of something falling to the sand.

She screamed. She did not turn to see whatever or whoever was there. She ran around the side of the house, flung the gate open, and ran across the street. She pounded on the door of the guest house. The matron, a heavyset woman about Jo's age, eventually opened the door. When she saw Jo, she raised a hand to her mouth and muttered, "I god."

Jo collapsed into the woman's broad, strong arms, sobbing.

❁

After the police had snooped around and left, Jo sat in her small, cramped living room with Rami, trying to relax. They'd searched the cottage high and low with all the lights burning; there had been no one hiding in the house. Or, if there had been, he was long gone, along with her camera, radio, several cassette tapes, and her purse, which held only her Peace Corps ID and twenty EC dollars. Jo sat on the love seat, legs folded beneath her. Rami sat with knees crossed in the chair opposite, smoking a cigarette. Between them, two candles burned dimly on the coffee table.

"Whoever it was, he probably thought you had a lot more goodies tucked away," Rami said. He leaned forward, looking for a place to tap his ashes. She pushed a heavy glass ashtray—a souvenir from her trip to Martinique—across the coffee table.

"It's because you're white, don't you see."

"I'm a target."

"Yes."

"I hate that feeling."

"I'm afraid it comes with the territory," he said, drawing deeply on his cigarette.

"If you make another crack about the white colonist, I'll throttle you."

"Then the police would have cause to visit this house a second time tonight." He smiled. "You wouldn't happen to have any liquor, would you? I fancy a stiff drink about now."

"Rum's on the kitchen counter, unless our intruder thought to grab that on his way out."

"May I pour you one?"

"Sure," she said. "I could use a nightcap." For a

moment she thought of asking for a cigarette, though she hadn't smoked since college. She knew that if she lit one now she'd never quit again.

He returned with two drinks. He handed her one and they clinked glasses.

"What are we toasting?"

He smiled. "How about a new house? If I were you, I wouldn't stay here."

"No way," she said. "I love this place. I'm not letting some asshole run me out. I'll do what that police officer said. Put a heavy piece of doweling in the track of the patio door. Get my landlord to install a good deadbolt in the kitchen and block the windows with plywood. I'll be safe as milk."

Rami frowned. "Rancid simile."

"And I'll get a dog."

"Sound plan. Woof woof."

She leaned back in the love seat and laughed; it felt good. She was glad he'd agreed to stay with her. The thought of make-up sex briefly tantalized her. The modest thrill of making love anyplace other than his apartment.

"I like you when you're chipper."

"I'm trying to cheer you up."

"You're not angry about tonight?"

He shook his head. "No. Just . . . disappointed."

"In whom?"

He lifted his eyebrows as he sucked on his cigarette.

They were quiet for several minutes. She missed her radio. She wanted to hear something soft, quiet, relaxing. Joni's *Blue*, perhaps.

"Why didn't your wife come with you?"

He was quiet for so long she thought he was ignoring

the question. And that was fine; she resolved to let it go once and for all. Things die. Let them.

"The official version," he answered, finally, "is that our two boys go to a very good school in Georgetown. My wife doesn't place much confidence in the Grenadian schools. You could say she is old-fashioned in some ways. She resisted moving from Guyana to anyplace other than America or the UK. She has ideas about Georgetown. About raising her family in a capital city. About being a doctor's wife, you see. She is like you: a strong woman. Very determined. She was raised in Georgetown. The poorer areas of our region . . . It would be a bit of a step down, you see. For her, it is a point of honor." He shook his head. "Her father is just a bureaucrat, a low-level civil servant. He has no connections. No power. Yet she is proud."

Jo sipped her rum. She was finally coming down from the excitement, and felt the drowsiness slowly rising. Rami seemed quiet.

"Hey," she said, "if this isn't—"

Rami slapped his knee. "The woman doesn't have the first idea! There are no jobs for doctors in Georgetown!" He drank his rum. "Do you know what I was doing before I accepted this post on Carriacou?"

"Private physician?"

He laughed. "I wish. I wish our family had that kind of money and influence. It is difficult to set up a private office in the city. Things are very corrupt. No," he said, setting his empty glass noisily onto the table, "I worked in my brother's dry goods shop. Apparently a clerk in Georgetown has more dignity than a doctor on Carriacou."

She sipped her drink. "You should tell her how people regard you here. The doctor's wife would be a big fish in a small pond."

"She'd laugh at the idea." He stood and walked into the kitchen, returning with the rum bottle. He poured himself two fingers. "Do you know she won't even allow the boys to visit? She thinks everyone here is small-minded. Backward. Stupid."

"I'm sorry. It must be tough."

"It's humiliating, you know? To have your wife say these things to you. And Sari is sharp-tongued, I assure you. She spares me nothing." He swished his drink in his hand, then threw it straight back.

"I resolved to quit that woman when I came here. I am through with her, Jo."

She bit her lower lip, gently. "Divorce?"

He shook his head. "She'd never have it. And I don't intend to press the matter. It would only harm the boys." He blew his nose into a handkerchief. "Harm them more. It's enough for their father to have left them."

"You'll be back in March."

"Only to leave again in May. I've taken a position with the Red Cross in Castries, St. Lucia. Renewable one-year contract, that sort of thing."

"Oh," she said. "Congratulations."

"Thank you," he said, flatly. He poured himself more rum.

"Why didn't you tell me?"

"About my marriage?" He rubbed his thumb along the lip of his glass. "It doesn't concern you, my dear. We're lovers, not confidantes."

She smiled, though the words stung. "I meant your job in St. Lucia."

"I'm leaving this island in March, regardless of where I go next. What possible difference could it make to you? We're now speaking frankly, of course."

"Yes. Isn't it wonderful."

He ground out his cigarette and immediately lit another. "How did you find out I was married?"

"It was a hunch," she said, sipping her drink. Suddenly, she didn't want the rum.

"No it wasn't," he said, sharply. "Someone told you."

"Or you told someone. But you didn't tell me." She set her glass on the table. She'd had enough to drink. She felt tired now, ready for sleep. "I guessed, Rami. That's all."

He frowned. "What gave it away?"

"The tan line on your ring finger," she said, standing.

He held his hand near the candle, turning it over and over.

"Just kidding." She exaggerated a yawn. "I'm going to bed now."

She gave herself a cat bath in the bathroom sink. She was too tired for a shower. While she now resented Rami's presence, she was too scared to stay alone without a lock on the door, and she couldn't see leaving the house open while she stayed anyplace else. With anyone else.

She could be anyone. A lover, not a confidante.

In the living room, she took down her hide-a-bed and then set Rami up on the couch with the spare bedsheets and a pillow. She saw that he'd had another glass of rum, and heard it in his voice as he argued with the tricky bathroom door. It was warm in the house. She switched the lights off, then stripped to her panties and bra and climbed under the sheets.

He was in the bathroom for several minutes. She heard coughing, then a gag. Was he vomiting? He hadn't had that much rum. Here. Who knew how much he'd had back at his place. The bathroom door opened and the light switched off. He stumbled against her dining table on his way across the room.

"Jo?"

"Yes."

"Where are you?"

"I'm in my bed."

"I can't see."

"Your eyes will adjust. Are you okay?"

"I'm lonely."

"I know."

"Let me come over."

"No," she said. "Sleep on the couch."

There was a long silence. His darkened silhouette stood in the middle of the room, unmoving.

"Rami?"

"Jo, I'm coming over there."

"No, you're not. If you do, I'll scream." She sat up in bed, drawing the sheet over her chest. "I'm serious. If you can't behave, get the hell out."

She gripped the bedsheet. The closest blunt object was the ashtray on the coffee table. She'd reach for it, if she had to.

He shuffled slowly to the couch.

Staring into the blackness above her, she listened

patiently to his groans and mumbles. His breathing gradually slowed and faded until, several minutes later, he began to snore. She rolled over on one arm and closed her eyes for sleep.

As a girl growing up in the suburbs of Minneapolis, she'd often wondered if anyone could ever live a full life—all of its pleasures and pains, victories and defeats—in a single day. It was the stuff fairy tales were made of, she knew that even as a girl. No single day could ever be enough.

Every single day contained too much.

She woke to the sound of someone rapping at her kitchen door. She sat up slowly in bed. The clock read eight. Impossible, she thought. She never slept that late. But then the memory of last night's troubles hit her. They'd been up late. And then all that rum. The rapping grew louder.

"Jo!" a voice shouted.

"Just a minute!"

Rami rolled over on the couch. "Oh, my head," he groaned. "Don't shout, damn it."

She got up and ran to the bathroom. She couldn't wait. The rapping came again.

"Stop, damn you!" Rami shouted. "She's coming."

She washed her hands, then quickly dressed in shorts and a clean T-shirt. As she walked into the kitchen she wondered if she'd swept all of the broken glass from the floor. She opened the door to find Cap holding up a small plastic bag of scotch bonnet peppers.

"Mummy send these for you," he said, grinning.

"Oh, Cap," she said, accepting the bag. "That's so nice."

"You like de hot pepper? I help grow dem meself."

"I do."

"Who in hell are you?" Rami said, stepping into the kitchen. He was bare-chested, wearing only his blue jeans. His hair was uncombed and he had dark circles under his eyes.

"This is Cap," Jo said. "A new friend."

"Friend," Rami sneered. "What you doing around here?"

"Ah bring de white lady a pepper, sah."

"You're a damn thief!" Rami snapped, bumping into Jo as he charged out the door. Cap took a step back as Rami swung at him, but with his bad leg, he couldn't move fast enough. Rami's blow caught him squarely on the side of the head, and sent him sprawling to the sand.

"Rami!" she shouted. "Stop it!"

He kicked at the boy as he struggled to get up. Damp morning sand covered one side of Cap's face.

"You damn vagrant. Don't come around here anymore!"

Jo grabbed Rami's arm. "Stop!" she shouted. "He's not the thief."

Cap ran as quickly as he could around the side of the house, a look of terror on his face. She knew she'd never see the boy again.

Rami tugged his arm free from her grip.

"What in hell did you do that for?"

"Why do you let that little street rat hang around here? You think he's being nice to you? He's studying your house, checking what you have."

"No," she said, "you're wrong."

He turned and gave her a fierce scowl. "What do you know, eh? You think you know this place? These people?"

She set her jaw tight. "Get your shirt and go."

He brought his hands up against the sides of his head and rubbed his temples vigorously. "Ahh," he groaned, smacking himself. He cursed again as he stepped inside.

She folded her arms across her chest and walked slowly out into the yard. A large coconut lay at the foot of the nearest palm tree. She picked it up. Brushing sand from the husk, she turned it over, looking for cracks. There were none. She smiled. She would have fresh coconut milk with her breakfast.

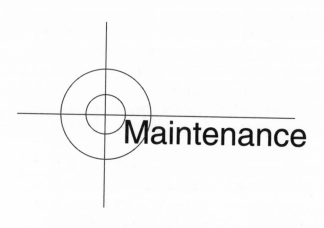

Maintenance

I recap the flask after taking a swig, then slip it into the thigh pocket of my work pants. I pick up the roller, wet it with paint, and push it along the seam joining ceiling and wall. I like the rhythm of dipping the roller into the paint, pushing it back and forth, covering up the old, spreading the new until it becomes seamless, bright and clean. It is order, it is maintenance, and it is essential.

This morning I'm out front of number seven, Dave's apartment, painting over his door frame. I work the roller carefully around the wood, leaving as little unpainted space as possible, so brushwork will be minimal. Slow, even footsteps in the stairwell break my concentration. I look down and see Dave's bright red hair. I am just finishing the last passes with the roller as he reaches the top of the stairs.

"Done here in a second. Hang on," I say.

He stands and watches me. "You know, I admire you," he says. "How you work with your hands. You're so patient."

"It's not much. I just do it to help with the rent." I set the roller in the tray, then slowly climb down the stepladder.

"But I respect that," says Dave. "I wish I could use my hands. I get so sick and tired of reading all the time." He holds up a brown folder. "Thirty-six freshman essays. Sometimes I wonder why I'm in graduate school."

I move the stepladder away from his doorway, then roll back the tarp from his door. I make a mock flourish with my hands. "There you go, sir."

"Thanks," he says, stepping up to his door. "Doesn't the smell get to you?"

"Nothing gets to me," I say.

At 4:15 I drain the last sip from my flask. A good time to wrap it up for the day, I think. I empty the tray of paint into the can, then reseal the can. I push the ladder and the tarp to the side of the hallway, so people can get by. I drop the brushes and the roller into a jar of water. I'll come back to clean them after I get a drink. I'll finish this floor tomorrow, then start on the next. Then there's the back stairwell, the basement, and in spring, the outside trim.

Before walking upstairs I turn around and examine my work. The difference, it seems to me, is remarkable. In fact, it's beautiful. I wish I'd found painting when I was about twenty-two, twenty-three. I could have saved a lot of time.

I sit in my kitchen, eating a sandwich, drinking whiskey and scanning the realty section of yesterday's paper. I would like to buy an apartment building, to own, operate, and maintain it. The problem is I don't have any money. I don't even have a job. B&G Software laid off half their technical documentation people six weeks ago. The severance pay is okay, but it won't last. I'm going to be on welfare for the first time in my life.

I wish Sarah would call, but she never does. She won't call because she's busy, busy lecturing, publishing articles, correcting essays. It's what she wants. She's happy, and I envy her. I want to tell her how I'm doing, though I don't have anything new to say. I finish my drink and, on impulse, dial her office at the university. She's busy, but has a minute.

"So what's on your mind?" she asks.

"Do you know what's just around the corner?"

"That depends on where I am."

"You're in the same town as your husband."

"I am separated from my spouse," she says, coolly.

"Can we meet for lunch tomorrow?" I ask.

"Why?"

I get the feeling she's talking to me on the side while arranging papers or marking an essay. "To talk," I say, quietly.

"Neil, do you need money again?"

"No, it's not that."

"So what is it? You're not drunk, are you?"

"Thanksgiving. Next Thursday is Thanksgiving." I hear voices and footsteps in the background of her office.

"You want to celebrate. Together, is that it?"

She makes it sound so foolish, I say, "Well, maybe not celebrate. Christ, I haven't seen you in two months. We don't have to talk about the past. We could just spend some time together."

"Sort of write off the first seven years?"

"If you like."

"I like. Listen," she says, "I have a meeting now. I have to go."

"What about lunch?"

"I don't know. I thought we weren't talking again until you'd dried out."

"It's not the kind of thing I can . . . Look, Sarah, what about Thanksgiving?"

"Neil," she says sternly, "now isn't the time for this. I really have to go, okay?" She disconnects.

The day begins slowly. I am on the couch. I roll over, onto my back. Nausea swells, then slowly fades. The sun pours its glaring light through my front windows, into my eyes, and straight to the back of my skull, where it feels like two sticks being jabbed through my eye sockets. How many drinks? The bottle is nearly empty, on the floor.

The pounding in my head is overwhelming. What I need are several glasses of water, some aspirin, and a trip to the bathroom. But I know it's much more than this. Sarah's right. I need help. I need to lay off. But I've said that a million times. I've got to call her and ask her to take me to a clinic.

I dial the house. It rings for a long time. A young man's voice answers, sleepily. I ask for my wife. I hear muffled conversation, then Sarah comes on.

"Why are you calling me at this hour on a Saturday?"

"Student?"

"What?"

"Teacher's assistant?"

She hangs up.

Outside it is very cold and a brisk breeze keeps my ears and cheeks tingling. An early snow has fallen, lightly covering everything. I turn to look at the trail of my footsteps. I am weaving. I assure myself that in a few hours, when the sun is high, all this will melt.

In the window of the diner is a sign advertising what I have come for. The Hangover Special: two eggs, meat, toast, choice of vodka screwdriver or Bloody Mary. $4.99.

I order the Bloody Mary.

When I get home there is a message on my answering machine.

"Neil. This is Sarah. Call me when you get up."

Her voice startles me. I want a drink, but I tell myself to wait. I haven't even taken my coat off yet. I sit down and listen to the message again, just to make sure I heard it right, then call. She answers.

"Are you free tonight?" she asks.

"Yes."

"I'd like to talk. Can we meet at La Terrasse at six? My treat."

"Sure," I say. "What's the occasion?"

"We'll talk," she says. "Do you need a ride?"

"No," I say. "I can get there."

"Are you sure? I could pick you up."

"No," I repeat. "See you at eight."

"Six," she says.

"Six, right."

In the kitchen I question why I said I didn't need a ride. I mix a drink, then another.

As I paint the third-floor hallway, the soft, squishy sound of the roller mellows the pounding in my head, relaxing me. It's like the sound of ocean waves or a distant thunderstorm; it's a peace you can't buy, period.

In the shower I meticulously scrub all the tiny white dots of paint from my arms. I shave. I put on a coat and tie, something I hope Sarah will like. She and I last ate at La Terrasse five years ago, to celebrate her winning tenure. It suddenly seems like a long time ago.

I go across the hall and ask Dave to lend me his car.

"Sorry," he says. "Going out tonight."

"Could you drop me at La Terrasse?" I ask. "It's a special occasion, sort of. My wife wants to treat me to a nice meal." This does not impress him. I remind him that I lent him my blender for his Halloween party and he still hasn't returned it.

"Calling in the debts," he says. "But I guess I have time. Give me five minutes."

In the car we talk about Thanksgiving. He says he'll probably spend it with people from the English department, fellow graduate students. It'll be just like Halloween. They'll talk, eat, drink, watch videos.

"What about you?" he asks.

"Ask me after dinner," I say.

"La Terrasse," he says. "Fancy. I don't see you in a tie very often. It's becoming."

"I don't know," I say. "I'm getting pretty used to those painting clothes."

"Sure. But it's good to do something different once in a while. Or that's what I'm telling myself." Dave pulls up to the restaurant. "I'm going on a blind date tonight. One of those ads in the paper." He laughs. "I can't believe I'm so desperate."

I am in the lounge at twenty to six. I sit in the corner of the dim room at a cocktail table for two. I sip scotch. Most of the people here look over fifty, with gray hair, pot bellies, sagging bosoms, and gold. Alone, I feel conspicuous.

At five past Sarah comes in. She is wearing a new black evening dress, and she looks stunning. Her shoulder-length black hair is pulled back tight in a ponytail. I'm struck by the luminous shine of her rich, olive skin, the slim, determined line of her jaw, the curve of her hips. Her dark eyes.

I stand to greet her. I'm hoping she will let me kiss her on the cheek. I would like that. She stops behind her chair. We say good evening, then sit. A waiter comes over. She announces our reservation and orders a bottle of red wine. When the waiter leaves, she turns to face me.

"So," she says, "we're looking a little worse for wear."

"Are we?" I ask.

"Wouldn't you say it's about time for a haircut?"

I shrug my shoulders. "This is a hell of a way to begin

an evening together," I mumble. I wrap a tangled curl of my hair around my finger, then release it. "And besides, I don't care."

"I know," she says.

The waiter brings her wine and states that our table is ready when we are.

"Fine," says Sarah. Her movements are precise, controlled. She radiates calm. I understand that she has mapped out a course for how this evening will go. She's probably outlined speeches in her mind. And I know, more or less, what she will say. There are things she wants me to say. There are things I won't tell her because it would be pointless. I know it's the same for her.

She begins to tell me about the school term, of her freshman art history survey course, of some bright students. She does not mention any names. She says she published an article on the Pre-Raphaelites. It got good reviews. I wonder if the sleepy voice is a freshman, who seduced who, then tell myself to ignore it. Although I have been faithful to our marriage, there was no reason to be.

We move into the dining room, which is cavernous and filled with the steady murmur of dinner table conversation. The chandeliers throw a dim, golden light about the room, which is done in dark wood and deep red. It's lush, comfortable.

After ordering, she asks me about my job hunt. I tell her about the deal with my landlord, about the painting. She's not really interested. It's too remote for her, too different from what she knew me as. But I tell her it all, anyway.

It is over the appetizer, spinach soup, that she begins.

"You're wondering why I asked you to dinner," she says, looking at her soup. She pauses, then says, carefully, "I don't think this will come as any great surprise. I want a divorce." She looks up at me, eyebrows raised. I realize I'm holding a spoonful of soup immobile at chest level. I swallow the soup and put the spoon down. "Well?" she asks.

"I have something to tell you," I say. The waiter brings a basket of rolls. I take one and begin to butter it, slowly. It is chewy, warm. I like these rolls.

"Yes?"

"I was back in my hometown," I begin, "back on the block I grew up on. All the houses, the sidewalks, everything. The trees. It was all right there."

"What the hell does that have to do with anything?" she asks.

"I gradually come to realize there are no people. No one. It's like the whole place is abandoned. There's a mower in Mr. Gordon's front lawn. He left it half-mowed. My dad's Buick is in the driveway. A bicycle leans against a tree. People's things are everywhere, but there's no people."

She sighs and leans back in her chair. "Oh, Jesus Christ."

"I try my house. It's unlocked. But again, it's empty. So is Gordon's. So is Carlyle's. Everyone's place is unlocked, like they all went somewhere in a hurry. I begin to walk the streets. I'm not seeing anything. No birds, no dogs, no squirrels. A total absence of animate life. I go over to the mini-mall they put in on Fourth Street. The K-Mart is locked. So is Beeglemeyer Foods.

"Paranoia sets in. Where could everyone be? What bizarre thing could have happened? What did I miss? I cross Thompson Park, walk behind the police station, head downtown. All these familiar places, yet it's like I'm in alien country. The wind is blowing dust and paper down the avenue. I stop and sit on a bench at a bus stop, across from a camera store, and I start thinking. This is just like *Omegaman*, where that guy is the last living human, and he has to fight off all the zombies that come out after dark, calling for him. Calling for his flesh."

"Is there a point to this?" Sarah asks.

"Suddenly, down a side street, I see a shop open. I can see the sign. 'Come in, we're open.' It's Tommy's Liquors.

"When I was growing up, in high school, me and my friends, we'd go to Tommy's to buy six-packs or pints of schnapps. He never checked for an ID, you know? We used to laugh at him, this fat old guy sitting in his musty little store.

"Well, Christ, am I glad he's there now. I run over to the shop, step inside, and there he is. A bit older, maybe fatter, but still the same red-faced old coot crammed in with the bottles and cigarettes.

"I say, 'Boy, am I glad to see you! Where is everyone? What happened? Why is the town empty?'

"His eyes are bleary. He stands with a grunt and grabs a bottle of scotch down off the shelf. He slips it into a paper bag, twists the top of the bag just so, and hands it to me. Then he sits down and resumes staring at the wall.

"It's clear to me that I'm supposed to leave, so I do. And that's it. There's nobody else in the whole damn town. I've just got this bottle."

Sarah pours herself another glass of wine. "The end?" she asks.

"The end."

"And just what was that?"

I push my wine glass forward for a refill. "You tell me."

She frowns. "It's a metaphor for your alcoholism," she says, watching my glass as she pours. "Hardly a metaphor."

"There's more to it, I think. It's the image of Tommy that haunts me. He's isolated, too, but he does nothing, wonders nothing. It's like he doesn't even notice it."

"A warning to you," says Sarah.

The steak is superb. So is the wine. Sarah tells me about the house, what she's done to it over the summer and fall, what shape it is in for winter. After this she asks about my apartment. It's simple, I tell her. One bedroom. She wouldn't like it.

After a short pause in the conversation, she says, "I want to go back to what I said earlier. We're beating around the bush. We need to discuss this."

I thoughtfully chew a piece of meat, savoring the juices.

"Don't you have anything to say?" she repeats.

I ask Sarah if she'll share another bottle of wine with me. She looks at the nearly empty bottle on our table. Her face is somber. Our meal is almost finished.

"No. I don't need it, and neither do you," she says. "I

have to drive home." She looks down at her plate, where she is carving her meat into small pieces. "Neil, why are you resisting me?"

She attempts to discuss the divorce one last time over cheesecake. I tell her I've been scanning the paper for a good apartment building. I want something small, four units, maybe six or eight. Something I can manage and maintain on my own. She resigns herself with a sigh and lets me ramble on. When I'm done talking she leans over her plate.

"Well, I don't know. For some childish reason you refuse to discuss this divorce with me. You're acting like an ass, but you can have it your way tonight. Just remember that my mind is set, and as far as I'm concerned, it's up to the lawyers now." She stands. "I'll pay the bill up front. Do you have a ride home?"

I take a packet of artificial sweetener from the small dish at our table, rip it open, and pour its contents on my dessert plate.

"Oh, to hell with you," she snaps, and walks off.

I take another packet of sweetener and pour its contents onto my plate. I repeat this action methodically until I have depleted the small dish. I am aware that other diners, bewildered, are observing this.

At the front the maitre d' asks me how the meal was.

"Superb," I say.

"Wonderful," he says. He is a short man, balding and gray over the ears. He sat us at our table. He wished us a happy meal. I imagine he has pieced together my whole sordid life. I reach for a toothpick beside the cash register.

"Are you married?" I ask.

He breaks out with a wide, sincere smile. "Yes. Twenty-seven years last August."

I pick at some beef lodged between my molars. "Hell of a thing," I mumble.

"Sir?" he asks, quizzically.

"Would you call me a cab?"

"Certainly, sir. You'll be in the lounge?"

Yes, how well this man knows me.

During the taxi ride home I am glum, pensive. The driver, an Italian who says his name is Duke, is trying to make small talk about the NFL season. His team is Green Bay, but they're out of it, he says. He figures it will be San Francisco again.

"Again," he repeats emphatically, pounding the palm of his hand on the steering wheel. "God damn them."

Again, I think. It's snowing again. In a few years the hallways will be cracked, peeling and dirty, and will need to be painted again.

"Stop by Lou's Liquors on the way home," I blurt out.

I meet Dave at the front door of our apartment building.

"Home so early?" I ask, fishing for my keys. "What happened to your date?"

"Not my type," he says, opening the door with his keys. We walk the stairs together, slowly. "How's your wife?" he asks.

"Not my type," I say.

This makes him laugh. On the second floor Dave bids me goodnight and begins to unlock his door. I pause on my way upstairs, then turn to look at him.

"Do you drink scotch?" I ask.

His door is halfway open. He smiles. "Yes."

"Would you like a drink?"

He shrugs his shoulders, relocks his door, and says, "Sure."

He follows me upstairs, and I usher him into my living room. "Take a seat," I say, pointing at the worn yellow chair in the corner of the living room. Our apartments are identical in layout, though mine is more frugal. I set the bottle on the trunk that serves as my coffee table. I bring out some soda, two glasses and ice. After mixing the drinks, I hand him his.

"Cheers," I say.

"Cheers."

We sip our drinks in an awkward silence, then Dave asks me how long Sarah and I have been separated. I tell him.

"Has it been hard?" he asks.

"Yes."

For some reason I don't mind telling him this. He's quiet, as if studying me. There's a relaxation about him, a relaxation that begins to wash over me. He continues to ask me simple questions. How long have we been married? Where did we meet? What was our wedding like? I find it easy to divulge these things without feeling embarrassed. I get the feeling he really wants to know, he really cares. After a couple more drinks I recline on the couch, still rambling on, emptying my guts. And I can't stop. It's as if his first few questions tapped a vein that is now flooding uncontrollably.

Soon I am into a monologue about the last couple of years, about the drinking and the arguments and the weekends spent alone at the YMCA before she finally sent me packing. I tell him about the time I rang the doorbell at three in the morning, drunk, and she wouldn't let me in, and how I stood in the front yard, screaming, until she finally called the police. Now it's over, I tell him. I've lost Sarah for good. And the hell of it is, I just let her go. I just sat back and let it all go.

I'm not sure exactly when it was that Dave left the yellow chair and came to sit on the floor next to me, nor do I remember exactly how I felt when he first began to stroke the hair on my head. I just remember it all felt right, it all somehow fit in, and I just kept talking, talking, talking.

Barnstorming

Jay lowered the binoculars and handed them across the table to his cousin, Laurie. She set them lens-down on the tablecloth, the silver bracelets around her wrist jangling. Her black hair hung in a long, thick ponytail over the front of her left shoulder. In the dusky light of late July her deeply tanned skin looked smooth, as if drinking in the shadows.

They sat on the front porch of a professor's geodesic dome, perched on a river bluff overlooking the Mississippi, Highway 61, and the Soo Line tracks running north to St. Paul: three pathways lined up neatly one beside the other, pavement and rails bending with the whims of the broad, blue river. They ate rotini with homemade tomato sauce and asparagus tips. A warm breeze blew up from the river valley. It was the best night of Jay's summer. Everything felt gorgeous.

"Wood thrush," he said, pointing to the giant oak that stood twenty feet from the front porch. "They're pretty common along the river. They like the shoreline marshes."

Laurie smiled, her lips pressed together. "Its song is beautiful. And you knew it, right away. How can you say you have nothing to show for your summer?"

"When did I say that?"

"Ten minutes ago." She drained the last sip from her glass. "You know something valuable about what surrounds you. Something beautiful."

Jay opened a second bottle of wine. "Yeah, well, beautiful doesn't pay the debts. I need money."

She frowned. "I don't think I can drive home now."

"You can sleep here. You know that."

"Are we still doing the picnic tomorrow?"

"I took off a Saturday from Frannie's. Best day for tips. We'd *better* be going on a picnic."

"Okay, okay. Just checking. I shouldn't drink too-too much if I'm going to fly tomorrow." She sat in the lawn chair with her skinny legs folded in a full lotus, twirling the stem of her empty wine glass between two fingers. "So how long are you going to wait tables at Frannie's? That place is such a dump."

Jay leaned forward and filled her glass. "I can't believe you've been. The only veggie thing you can order there is hash browns."

"It's the closest diner to the Paramount. If you want a slice of pie after the midnight movie, it's your easiest option."

"They use lard in the crust."

"Figures." She tucked a loose strand of hair behind her ear. "You didn't answer my question."

He drummed his fingers on the table and smiled. "What movie did you see?"

"Blue. It was only there for a weekend."

He poured himself a glass of wine, disappointed that she hadn't thought to call him. "Just my luck. One good thing comes to Red Wing and I miss it." He set the bottle between them. "Did you go alone?"

She laughed. "Now you sound like my mother."

"It's this country living. I have nothing better to do than sit around wondering what other people are doing." He crossed his feet at the ankles and stretched back in his chair. "I need a new plan."

Laurie smiled. "That makes two of us. I don't know where I'll be this time next month, but I can tell you it won't be Hastings, Minnesota. I've come home from Africa. I've visited the parental units. It's time to move on."

"The problem is, you're like me. You have no idea what to do."

She closed her eyes and tilted her head to one side. The breeze blew tendrils of hair across her lips and mouth, like fingers caressing skin.

He cleared his throat. "What if you could do anything?"

"Hmm." She opened her eyes and sipped her wine. "Anything?"

"Your wildest fantasy."

She lifted her chin and drew the tip of her finger slowly over her Adam's apple. "When I was sixteen I wanted so badly to be a barnstormer. You know, back in the old days when flying was still new and rare and people would travel just to see your plane, just to see you take it up into the air and do the rolls and flips and then return to earth. I'm not talking about air shows these days, with jets in formation and mock dogfights. I'm talking about one person in her biplane just bopping around the country, entertaining a handful of people at a time. Flying off into the sunset, alone. You used to be able to make a living at it."

Jay tapped the back of a book of matches with his thumb. "Faulkner has a novel about something like that. *Pylon.* I could lend it to you."

"A book?" She scrunched up her nose at him. The wrinkles around her eyes reminded him of his mother. "Is everything a damn book with you?"

He shrugged his shoulders. "Probably."

"Have you ever thought about graduate school? You know, in literature? Or is that too obvious?"

"No thanks," he said. He spilled a little wine on his chin and wiped it with a napkin. "I want to make money, not owe it."

"Owe more of it."

"Right." He tossed the napkin in a loose ball onto the table. Sometimes he thought she knew too much about him.

"Maybe I'll fly out to New Mexico and visit your mother," she said. "You could come."

"And be a dropout at the free love commune? I'll pass."

"I thought it was an organic farming collective."

"She's a Branch Davidian for all I know."

She gave him a long, hard look. "I'm serious."

"I know." He shifted in his seat.

She sipped her wine and raised an eyebrow. "Well?"

He rolled a piece of pasta back and forth with the tip of his fork. "Look, I know you like her. You like how mellow and easy-going she is. But it's another thing when you're her kid."

Laurie unfolded her legs and sat back in her chair. Her silence made him uncomfortable.

"My mother is a dropout. I don't need lessons in running. I need a direction, a goal. I've been thinking I could try to get back into editing. Or freelance writing."

"Let me tell you something about your mother," Laurie said, abruptly. "That woman's got it where it counts. She does what she wants, and she doesn't care who gets pissed off. You have to respect that."

"No, *you* have to respect that." He dropped his fork onto his plate with a loud clack.

A big yacht cruised slowly downstream on the river below, its cabin windows a warm yellow, its music pulsing and echoing off the bluffs. A man stood on the stern, singing along to "Roxanne," off-key. People on the boat laughed. Laurie craned her neck to see. Jay watched her quietly: her pale blue eyes, her slender nose, the scar on her left cheek that folded like a dimple when she smiled. He reached across the small table and touched the back of her hand, trailing a finger lightly across it. She turned to him. A faint smile crossed her face, lines just barely forming at the corners of her mouth.

He couldn't find the words. There had always been the danger of their intimacy. They'd never *done* anything, minus a little kissing one summer up at the lake cabin when he was thirteen. But the danger was always there, thick and unavoidable.

She turned back to the river. The yacht had passed them. He collected the dinner plates and took them into the kitchen, where he set them very quietly into the sink and poured hot tap water over them.

Once, after a bitter argument with his mother, Jay had threatened to leave home. He was fourteen years old.

His mother stood at the sink, peeling potatoes for a stew. Her knuckles were raw and red from the tap water. "Go for it," she said. "If you pack your suitcase right this instant, I'll drive you to the bus station and buy you a ticket anywhere you want to go."

They actually got as far as the parking lot of the Greyhound terminal in downtown Minneapolis. A big blue-and-white bus nestled the terminal, gray smoke chugging from the tailpipe. The banner over the windshield read CHICAGO. A man was slinging suitcases into the compartment beneath the seats. He treated the luggage roughly, Jay thought.

His mother sat smoking a cigarette, exhaling though the slit of the car window.

"Well, go on, little man. I'm not going to eat up a tank of gas while you make up your mind."

It was March and very cold. The car heater blew hot, dry air against his face. He had no idea where in the world he wanted to go. He didn't want to go, but he didn't want to stay. He didn't know what he wanted, and that made him feel even more miserable.

Several minutes later, the bus pulled out of the terminal. His mother ground out the cigarette in the ashtray. "Are you ready to go home now?"

"Yes," he said, his cheek pressed up against the cold glass of the car window.

They drove along the shiny black streets without speaking. The snowbanks lining Lyndale Avenue were dark with slush. Everything seemed gray and dull.

His mother pulled up to the curb in front of their apartment. She turned off the car engine but neither of them made any move to leave. The engine ticked softly.

"I was sixteen when I left my parent's house," she said. "I was as angry with life as you can get. My parents wanted me to do so many things, to act a certain way, to be the daughter they'd always dreamed of having." She gripped and released the steering wheel. "I wish I could say running was the best thing I ever did."

She turned to face him. The car seat creaked as she shifted her weight. "I'm never going to tell you what to do with your life. You make your own decisions, and you take the consequences. If you want advice, I can give you that. But don't ever expect me to tell you what to do."

"You would have let me get on that bus."

She brushed at his coat sleeve. "I was scared you'd do it. Just like your father, you know? We're all three of us going to be loners in this life."

Jay shivered. He wanted to go back inside the apartment. The windshield was beginning to frost over in the cold.

The back half of the professor's dome had been sectioned off into two bedrooms and a bathroom, on top of which was a loft. Jay liked it up there. It was Dr. Shelton's study, with a nice big desk and a huge dormer window facing west. And the books: every kind of field guide you could imagine, plus thick volumes on nesting patterns, migratory routes, anatomy, reproduction, diet, you name it. In the corner of the loft stood a metal cabinet containing his library of bird songs. Hundreds of cassettes, arranged alphabetically by the Latin names of the birds.

Jay brought down a tape of *Gavia immer*, the common loon, recorded in the Quetico in August 1985. He put the tape on the stereo. There was a bit of rustling and some muffled human voices. Then silence. He turned up the volume and returned to the porch. Laurie lay on the planks of the deck, staring up at the night sky. He reached inside and turned off the track lights in the living room and then sat down next to her. On the tape, thunder rose and fell like a kettle drum.

"What's this?" she asked.

"Shh." He held a finger to her lips. There was the sound of wind rustling through the trees, and then the long, plaintive call of a male loon.

She bit once at the tip of his finger. "Play *Abbey Road*. You were always such a Beatles nut."

"It's a field recording of loons. Shelton is an ornithologist. He records bird songs. He's got hundreds of tapes upstairs."

"Does he want the house sitter playing them?"

"Shh."

They listened quietly for a couple of minutes. Thunder, wind in the trees, loons. It was like an orchestra set loose without a conductor, drums and flute negotiating a slow dance between themselves.

Laurie suddenly burst out laughing, rolling onto one side and bringing her knees up to her chest.

"What?" he said, sharply.

"Hearing this reminds me of Grandma's cabin. Remember about Bigfoot?"

He shook his head slowly. But then he started laughing, too. A good, long, relaxing laugh.

The summer he'd turned eleven, his mom took him, Laurie, and Laurie's older sister Janet up to the family lake cabin for two whole weeks. As usual, he'd brought along a stack of books, all of them detailing his latest obsession: Bigfoot. This was all he wanted to talk about. One afternoon Laurie and Janet rushed into the cabin claiming they'd just found Bigfoot tracks. He ran with them down the long, sandy driveway out to the county road, breathless. There in the damp soil were the enormous prints, a foot long and half an inch deep. Just like in the books. He was dumbstruck. The tracks ran along the shoulder of the road for twenty feet before they veered off into a marsh full of cattails and reeds. He rushed back to the cabin and began pleading with his mom to drive to Duluth to buy some plaster of paris so he could form casts of the prints. Meanwhile, he'd organize a search party. His mom, sipping iced tea on the lawn, put up with this for an hour before demanding Janet tell him the truth.

He knew right then that they'd played him for a sucker. All of them. His mom and Laurie smiled fondly, but Janet burst out laughing. She was fifteen to Laurie's thirteen and his eleven, and had all but dubbed herself Queen of the Lake that summer.

"You're so retarded," she said. She had a sharp, insistent voice. She pushed him in the chest. "There's no such thing as Bigfoot, you moron."

"You're a moron!" he shouted. And in full view of his mother, he punched Janet in the stomach. She doubled over onto the grass, screaming shrilly.

"Jay!" His mother stood from her chair.

He sprinted down the driveway and out to the county road, running until his lungs burned. He stopped at the boat landing on the west side of the lake, where he sat under a white birch and threw stones into the water. He hadn't punched Janet *that* hard. But he knew it was wrong and he felt like a dope for caving in to her. Now he'd have to go back and apologize. The crummy bitch would win in the end. If he'd just been quiet *he* would've won. He'd remember that for a long time.

After a while he walked back to the cabin. He met Laurie at the top of the driveway. She said she'd been sent by his mother to tell him to come back right this instant.

"I'm coming," he said, miserably.

She grabbed his hand and squeezed it. "I'll tell her I couldn't find you."

He'd hugged her, pulling her tightly against his chest. He'd always remembered her thin body in his arms, the warmth of her skin, the sweet smell of her hair.

Loons called from the darkened living room.

He listened for Laurie's breathing and decided she was asleep before rolling onto his side and shutting his eyes.

At first Jay only played the tapes. He loved the bird songs. He'd play them when he got home from waiting tables at Frannie's. They calmed him down. *Gavia immer* was his favorite, but there were plenty of good ones. It wasn't until summer that he first started wondering about the birds, about the fact that there were so many of them out there, all around him.

He started with a pair of binoculars and a one-volume field guide. He sat on the front porch trying to spot birds in flight. He quickly realized that was pointless. Trying to follow, let alone identify, a flying bird with binoculars is next to impossible. He read a short essay on birding in one of the guides and then he knew what to do.

Shelton's dome was the only house on that particular ridge—the only house for a couple of miles, as far as Jay could tell. He hiked through the trees along the ridge to a large rock outcrop overlooking the river valley. He sat in the sun, trying to be very still like it said in the essay. It was frustrating. He saw so few birds, and the ones he did see he didn't recognize. He'd see one and start flipping through the field guide, frantically trying to identify it. The next thing he knew he'd been distracted for five minutes and the bird was long gone.

He learned that the thing to do was to keep watching. Take notes, if you must, but be brief. He studied the parts of a bird: the mantle, lore, and culmen. He learned where the primaries, scapulars, and tertiaries are on the wings. Distinguishing field marks are what to look for. Streaks of color on the bird's side. The color of the head in contrast to its back. The shape of the bill. After a couple of weeks he calmed down and became less obsessed with identifying every bird he saw. That was when it started to click. He began to recognize the more common species. He found he could distinguish between a jay, a thrush, and a swallow. He saw falcons soaring over the river. Young robins learning to fly. And he loved it. It was a matter of learning to appreciate what's put before you. There's nothing to do. No hunting or prowling or conniving. Just observe and appreciate. It's that simple. Later, when he got back to the dome, he'd dig out his notes and flip through the books and try to find what new birds he'd seen. But it didn't matter as much. He knew he'd see most of them again, sooner or later.

Birding took patience—more than he'd anticipated. But as the summer wore on he found he had more of that patience in him than he'd realized. He found himself spending more and more time combing the ridge. He hid in thickets, under big trees, on rock outcrops or under them. Just about anywhere he could go where he could comfortably sit still and go unnoticed for long periods of time. He considered himself good at that.

Saturday was perfect, with bright sunshine, clear blue skies, and a warm breeze Jay figured had to be good for flying. He watched as Laurie walked around her blue-and-white biplane, checking things and polishing the fuselage with a hand rag. She took a yellow motorcycle helmet from a small cargo hold behind the cockpit and handed it to him.

"Here. I've got this. See if it fits."

It didn't.

"Well, just hope I don't crash," she said, shrugging her shoulders. She strapped the helmet back in place and shut the cargo door.

"Do you ever wear a parachute?"

She laughed and patted his shoulder. "Sure you want to do the barnstorming bit? It's your first time up with me. I won't be offended."

"No, no, do it," he said. "Even if you hear me screaming bloody murder, just do it. I'll thank you later."

"You mean you'll strangle me later." She smiled and winked at him; that smile-and-a-wink combo was one of his mom's moves, one of her signatures. Laurie had it down cold, including the slight tilt of the head to the right. This struck him as less than reassuring.

She pointed to the rear cockpit. "Get in, cuz. Put your foot here, then here." She pointed to small metal footholds on the plane's side.

He climbed up and lowered himself slowly into the small, black vinyl seat. He hated her calling him "cuz." It was like a stop sign at a dangerous intersection. He strapped himself in with X-shaped chest belts and a waist belt. Laurie climbed into the front seat, behind the windscreen and all the controls.

"You bring sunglasses?"

"Yeah."

"Better wear them. The force of the wind."

She put on cat-eye Ray-Bans with a neon green elastic band running from ear to ear.

"Ready?"

"Let's do it."

She pulled a white helmet on over her head, secured the straps, then gave Jay a thumbs-up. The engine coughed and turned over once, twice—the entire plane shaking with the effort—before catching. Puffs of black smoke shot out from the engine cap and then the plane was vibrating with the rhythm of the engine. Jay shook from the base of his neck right down to the balls of his feet. Laurie checked the flaps on each wing, making them go up and down like a hand flexing at the wrist. Then the engine revved higher and the plane taxied, slowly at first, out onto the runway. The suspension felt stiff; every bump and jostle of the plane shot through his body like a strong slap on the back. The wings, the fuselage, the padding on his seat: everything seemed hopelessly, dangerously thin.

At the end of the runway they did a one-eighty and, without waiting, Laurie gunned the engine and they accelerated down the strip. Pressed back against his seat, Jay felt the tail rise like the back of a scared cat. He reached for the handles on either side of him, gripping them so tightly his knuckles turned bright white. Seconds later they were aloft, the ground dropping away from them rapidly, the wind blowing his hair straight back. He felt every dip and rise of the plane, felt it rock left and right. It seemed so puny and fragile, this biplane, like it might fall apart into a thousand tiny pieces at any instant. Who ever survived an airplane crash? But no—he had to trust Laurie. She knew what she was doing.

They climbed to four thousand feet and then the engine settled into a steady, quiet drone. They flew due east, toward the river. He studied the patchwork pattern of yellow-and-green fields divided by thin, dusty roads. He'd never before realized how hopelessly illogical, how scattershot it all appeared, as if laid out with no plan whatsoever. Oddly, this comforted him. He loosened his grip on the handles. A little.

A few minutes later Laurie drew a circle in the air with her finger. What in hell did that mean? Suddenly the engine revved and they were climbing, the nose rising like a second hand approaching twelve. Jay's stomach tightened and he gripped the handles again. He thought of slapping Laurie's shoulder and screaming "No! No!" But instead he gritted his teeth. He looked quickly over the side of the plane. Big mistake. Nothing between him and terra firma but a couple of lousy seatbelts.

The plane was losing speed, even though the engine was roaring at the same terrible pitch. It didn't feel right. Too risky. The plane continued to slow until it hung still for one awful second and then slowly, slowly fell back. For a moment, Jay felt weightless. Then they were spinning, out of control, the engine silent and the fields below twirling like a kaleidoscope. He felt dizzy and nauseous. The engine roared and they rolled to their right, the ground frighteningly close. G-forces pressed him back into his seat, pulling at his cheeks with a thousand tiny fingers. He squeezed the grips at his sides and let loose with a primeval scream that burned the back of his throat. His eyes watered from the force of the wind. And then he felt lighter and rose out of his seat for a moment, the straps digging into his shoulders. Land and sky spun clockwise around him, like a tunnel in a fun house: barrel rolls—an endless cycle of them.

When Laurie leveled off at a thousand feet the blood pounded in Jay's ears like timpani. They were over the Mississippi, the city of Red Wing spread out on their right like a messy breakfast table at Frannie's. And then Lake Pepin, with the water-skiers and yachts and wave runners cutting countless thin white wakes against the indigo water. He felt awake, totally alert and in the moment. The joy ride was over. He'd survived.

Laurie landed the plane on a dirt access road running between two pastures, scattering a herd of grazing milk cattle. She obviously knew the place but laughed when Jay asked where they were, who owned the land, how she knew about the spot.

"You're in Wisconsin," she said, as if that were all he needed to know.

"So should I expect some farmer with a shotgun to drive up in a truck in twenty minutes?"

She rolled her eyes. "Is it possible for you to live with even the slightest degree of mystery? Or to dream? Just for one day?" She opened the cargo door, took out a rolled-up blanket, and tossed it against his chest.

He took a step back as he caught it.

She took out a small plastic cooler, then shut the cargo door. "Now shut up and follow me."

They walked down a slight hill to a flat strip of land beneath a massive sugar maple. Crickets leapt from the tall grass as Jay spread the blanket. Laurie removed her boots and socks. They sat twenty yards from the Y-shaped confluence of two streams, one coming from the low hills to the west and the other from the flatter north.

"Okay, this is beautiful," he said.

"Exactly. Now dish out the food. I'm starved."

They ate their sandwiches and drank cold beer in cans. And for dessert, double-chocolate brownies—his mother's recipe. After lunch Jay took off his shirt and lay back on the blanket, listening to the burbling streams, his bare chest drinking in the warmth of the sun.

"What did you miss most about the States when you were in the Peace Corps?"

"Pro wrestling."

"Be serious."

"A warm shower. That was the only thing I never got used to." A moment later she added, "Africa seems so far away just now."

A deer fly landed on his forearm. He watched it hop left, then right, negotiating a space between his thick, black arm hair. Predictably, it bit him—sharp, insistent, painful. And, just as predictably, he slapped the fly with his other hand and killed it.

"Doesn't it ever bother you?" he asked. "Not knowing what's next?"

"Not right now, it doesn't."

Jay smiled. He felt hot, open, on the edge of something.

The warm breeze that blew across the pastures was dry and smelled sweetly of earth and manure. Jay woke slowly and opened one eye. A purple cornflower nodded and swayed in its own quiet rhythm amidst the more stolid stalks of prairie grass and thick, low weeds. Birds chirped softly from the tree above. He rolled over onto his right side. Laurie was not on the blanket beside him. Where was she? Up checking the plane? Off in the grass taking a leak?

A bird circled in the sky high above. He grabbed the binoculars and watched it drift along the currents, a solitary dark shape against the light blue afternoon sky. A kestrel, he was sure. They hunted the pastures for field mice. The falcon turned in a broad lazy circle, then darted out of view, diving off behind a distant line of trees.

Jay put on his sunglasses and stood. Laurie's blue jeans, socks, and boots were in a loose pile a few feet from their blanket. He stood on his tip-toes. She wasn't up by the plane. He walked around the sugar maple and into the grass, toward the stream. He found her there, thigh-deep in the water, her back to him. He watched her turn slowly at the waist, dragging her fingertips across the water's surface. Her T-shirt hung loosely around her upper legs, damp along the hem. He was about to call her when she bent over, submerging her arms up to her elbows. Her ponytail rolled over her left shoulder, the moving water grabbing at its tip, making it bounce. Her shirt rose up her backside, exposing the folds of her buttocks. Muscles flexed in the backs of her smooth legs as she swayed left and right, moving her arms through the water.

He watched her quietly, gently biting his lower lip.

He stripped to his boxers on the bank and stepped cautiously into the shallow blue stream. The rocky bed was firm. The clean, smooth stones dug into his feet, making him step carefully and slowly to be sure of his footing. Laurie moved out to the middle of the stream, her back still to him. Had she heard him? She submerged herself completely, remaining underwater for more than a minute. Jay stood still, the cold water cresting just over his knees. The blurry white form of her T-shirt under the shifting surface of the stream looked like smoke. And then her head rose slowly from the water, chin extended, eyes shut, black hair hanging straight back, shiny and wet. She turned to face him and gestured with her chin to the space beside her.

His stomach trembled with the cold as he waded out to her, every muscle tightening with the shock of the water on his groin. He let out a quick gasp as he bent forward, submerging his arms up to his shoulders. He didn't think he could do it—dunk and hold himself underwater. But there was Laurie, quietly watching him with those blue eyes, water beading along the underside of her jaw, her hair spread out behind her like a fan on the stream's surface. He took a deep breath and dropped straight down.

The water was so cold it hurt his eyelids. He held his breath as long as he could, trying not to move. He counted to thirty-three before he burst back to the surface, splashing water everywhere.

"Christ!" he bellowed, gasping for air. Something ran through the grass on the opposite bank, startled.

"Shh," whispered Laurie.

"But it's so fucking cold!"

"Don't think about the cold," she said, her voice even and soft. "Just be here."

She closed her eyes and remained absolutely still. He sank back down to his neck and tried his best to concentrate on the sound of the stream. The birds chirping in the grass. The distorted reflection of clouds on the water's surface. Laurie's skin, tight and bristling with gooseflesh. Anything but the cold.

"It feels good now, doesn't it?"

"I don't know."

A goldfinch landed on a tree stump just downstream, cocking its black eye and studying them quietly, its head darting rapidly.

"You should've waded in naked," she said.

"You didn't."

"I usually do."

The goldfinch let out a sharp *swee-swee,* then flew off.

"There's a beach on Cedar Lake I should take you to."

"I'm not a nudist," she said. "I won't do it with just anyone."

Jay's teeth chattered and his belly trembled.

"So who takes off their underwear first?"

She laughed. "I don't know if we should."

"Why not? We've gotten this far."

"No," she said, smiling. "I mean, I know you're freezing."

He swallowed and said nothing, his mouth suddenly dry. He wanted her to keep talking, for the spell of her voice not to cease.

"I'm warming," he said, finally.

She nodded, then rose from the stream, her wet, white shirt clinging to her back like thin gauze. She climbed onto the bank gracefully and stood, unshy, among the slender reeds and grasses, offering him her hand.

What We Leave Behind

Paul was ten minutes late. He sat quietly for a moment, watching tendrils of blue-gray smoke curl out from under the car's hood. The old Toyota was an oil burner, but it still got him from A to B. So what if the passenger-side seat had broken through the rusty floorboards last winter? If you've got a car, you've got options. It was important to remember that.

He opened the glove compartment, took out his plaid yellow tie, and pulled it over his head. He checked his hair in the rearview mirror, popped a mint in his mouth, and slid the knot up snug against the base of his throat. He kept thinking he had to pee, though he'd just peed a few minutes ago in the satellite at the practice range. It was just those damn Warner shows. It wasn't the nerves; he could handle nerves. You don't win three NCAA tourneys in two years if you can't handle nerves. Grades, that's another matter. It turned out he couldn't handle grades.

No, what he hated about the Warner shows was how every line and every action was scripted and prepared in advance. Nothing to do but go through the motions. Learn to do that with *heart*, his manager Dawn had said, and you'll be rich. Think of Yul Brynner, she said. He played the lead role in *The King and I* from 1951–1985, never once straying from his scripted lines. He died a millionaire.

The only motion Paul wanted to go through was a golf swing. He'd found the best way to kill time between Warner shows was to shoot range balls. Maybe he could become one of the Yul Brynners of golf: Arnold Palmer, Jack Nicklaus, Tom Kite. Guys who hit the same beautiful swing year after year after year. They were millionaires, too.

From the rear of his Toyota he took the white cardboard box containing the Warner display unit and his gray plastic briefcase. He pulled on his sport coat, which felt unbelievably warm and, because he hadn't dry-cleaned it in more than two weeks, smelled faintly of BO. He closed the Toyota's hatch. A few flakes of rust fell to the pavement at his feet. He locked the car—his three-year-old set of Pings were in plain view in the back—and walked slowly across the Copeland's front lawn. The brown grass was stiff under his loafers. The house looked nice enough: a small blue-and-white two-story, in need of a little paint and a good hedge trimming. Drapes covered the front windows. Paul crunched the mint in his mouth into tiny shards and told himself he was *hungry*. This was a sale. He imagined he already had the three-hundred-dollar commission in his hands. He imagined in a month, or two months, when he was finally selling three or four of these things a week, like Dawn had said he could. You have to *believe*, she said. You have to *want* it.

The front door was open, so he knocked on the screen door. He dabbed at his face with a handkerchief. He was still sweating from hitting range balls, plus he had to pee again. The street was quiet, drenched in sunlight. There weren't enough leaves on the trees yet for heavy shade. A girl rode down the avenue on her bike, her long blonde pigtails flapping behind her in the breeze. He heard the *click-a-click-a-click* of the bike's gears as she pedaled. Smooth and rhythmic—going through the motions.

Mrs. Copeland came to the door barefoot, wearing a close-fitting navy T-shirt tucked into khaki shorts. A white belt was cinched tightly around her waist. Her gray-black hair was cut short, like a boy's. He figured her for about fifty.

She gave him a quick once-over, then leaned a shoulder against the door frame. "You're not a Mormon, are you?"

Paul laughed. "Lapsed Catholic. And that's being generous."

"Figures. A Mormon would never wear a tie like that."

He grinned and picked up the tie between two fingers and flapped the end around. "Too loud and crazy?"

"Too something," she said, smiling. "So who are you?"

"I'm Paul Hammond, from the Warner company. You won a free carpet shampoo, remember? We spoke on Monday."

She bent over a little to one side to scratch the back of her leg. Her forearms and legs were thin—the kind of thin that gets you wondering.

"What're you selling?"

He took a small green card from his coat pocket and held it up.

"Mrs. Copeland, you've won a free gift. Remember that contest you entered? You signed this card."

From her shorts pocket she took a pair of reading glasses with narrow, rectangular lenses. She lifted her chin and read the card, then looked down at the box and suitcase at his feet. She removed the glasses and put them back in her pocket.

"Thought I signed up for a grocery giveaway."

"That's right, you did. And you're still registered for that giveaway, which will be next month. In the mean-time, you've won a free carpet shampoo. How about it?"

She furrowed her brow and ran a finger along the top of her shorts, as if checking to make sure the belt was in place and her shirt was still tucked in.

"How come you're sweating so much? I don't know if I should trust you."

He smiled. "It's hot, Mrs. Copeland." He took the handkerchief from his coat pocket and dabbed his face. He pretended to wring it out before putting it back in his pocket. She actually laughed.

"Sandy," she said, opening the screen door. "Come in and get yourself a drink, Paul. You look like you could use one."

The house was warm and a bit musty smelling, like she'd opened the windows for the first time that day, after the long Minnesota winter. He set his briefcase and display unit in the front hallway. His shirt was already sticking to his back.

"What's your fancy? The fridge is full."

He shrugged his shoulders. BO wafted up to his nose. "Water would be fine."

"Tssk," she said, shaking her head. "You're no fun."

He followed her down a short hallway and into a small kitchen-dining area. The table was piled with coupons and a week's worth of the *Star-Tribune*. A window looked out onto a narrow back yard of brown grass, bordered by a tall wooden fence. A rusty old Weber with one bent leg stood in the middle of the yard.

Sandy came out from the kitchen with a tall glass of water and handed it to him. He said thanks and took a drink. He was trying to think of what to say next.

"Front talk sets up the sale," Dawn had told him. "No front talk, no sale." She was full of little sayings like that. "ABC" was another one: "Always be closing." Dawn believed in these sayings, Paul could tell from the excited way she spoke. She'd jab at the air in front of her as if she were digging her finger into your chest, pacing like a cat across the front of the room as she talked. She'd slam the podium as she fired off questions. She got so worked up, the back of her blouse had a damp spot between her shoulder blades. Dawn was a believer. When she talked, Paul felt his life was not completely off track. If he wanted it badly enough, he could turn it all around.

He drank the rest of his water in two greedy gulps, then wiped his mouth on his coat sleeve. If just one of his college professors had been as hyper as Dawn, he might've gotten a degree, instead of the "Withdrawn—Failing Grades" notice the university had mailed him a few weeks after he'd left.

"Thanks," he said again, setting the glass on the table.

"Hey, it's just tap water, kid. Drink as much as you want. Minnesota's the land of ten thousand lakes, right?"

"Yeah," he said, laughing. He went to the sink and refilled his glass, then rejoined her in the dining area.

"So how much carpet do you clean on this deal?" Her fingers were wrapped around the lip of a tall glass of something clear and fizzy, with a twist of lime in it.

"One room."

"Come on and I'll show you the one, then."

He followed her into a sunken, rectangular living room directly off the dining area. A coffee table stood in front of a long couch, next to which was a recliner, its footrest fully extended. There was a patio door and a TV on the left. Paul set his demo unit and briefcase on the floor near the patio door.

Sandy picked up a lit cigarette from a glass ashtray on the coffee table, knocked off about an inch of ashes, and took a long drag. He wanted to ask her if she'd mind him lighting up, but figured he should wait.

"This is it," she said, waving a hand around the room.

Above the mantle hung a painting of a huge mansion, built of gray stone. A tall set of bay windows in the middle of the first floor looked out over a flat, green lawn. The sky overhead was blue, but heavy, gray clouds were building along the horizon. Up on the second floor of the mansion, on the right-hand side, was an enormous clock with its hands at 12:45. That clock blew Paul away. Why would a guy build a mansion like that and then put a damn clock in it? But as he looked at the painting a little more, he began to recognize things. That clock, for one. On second thought, he was sure he'd seen it before. And that lawn in front of the mansion: it had a sluice or ditch running across it, with this funky little arched stone footbridge. Then it hit him, and he felt like an idiot: it wasn't a mansion and that wasn't a lawn.

"That's St. Andrew's, isn't it?"

"What?"

"That painting. It's the clubhouse at St. Andrew's, in Scotland. It's where golf was invented." He dabbed at his face again with his handkerchief. He needed to take his coat off. "I've always wanted to play that course."

She frowned. "You're a golfer."

He nodded. "I had a scholarship to the U. For a while, anyway. I'm playing the amateur circuit in the upper Midwest this year. I'll turn pro in a year, maybe two at the most."

"Pro golf. Really?"

"Yeah," he said, smiling and bobbing once on his toes.

"That's a shame. You look like a nice kid." She took a drag off her cigarette. She pointed up to the painting. "If that's what Scotland looks like, count me out. All those rotting old mansions standing alone in the fields? Too dreary."

"I guess it rains a lot in Scotland."

She bent down and ground her cigarette out forcefully. "Honey, it rains a lot no matter where you are. You ought to know that by now."

Paul nodded slowly. "Sure, I know that."

She picked up her pack of Virginia Slims and lit another cigarette, then cleared her throat. Her eyes were bloodshot, and she had dark circles under them.

"So, you going to clean this carpet, Paul, or what?"

"You bet." He took off his coat and set it in a corner, then bent down on one knee. He ran a hand over the carpet, felt the nap. The gesture didn't mean anything, but it made him look like he knew what he was doing. What he knew about that carpet: it was red, maybe maroon. It was pretty old and beat up, with obvious wear patterns near the steps and the patio door. The room was small. It would only take about forty-five minutes to shampoo, rinse, and buff—with a long smoke-break in the middle.

"I guess you don't have to worry about cleaning under the furniture. It never moves." She laughed.

"If we could just move this coffee table, that'd be good."

Together they pushed the table in front of the fire-place.

"This'll have to do you," she said. She leaned over and popped the lever on the recliner, which snapped shut quickly. "Like I said, if you want something to drink, the fridge is yours. Let me know when you're done." She turned to walk out of the room.

"If you don't mind, I'd like to take just a bit of your time to show you our product. To give you an idea of what we'll use to clean your carpet."

She frowned. "I don't care what you use to clean the carpet. It's free, right?"

"Absolutely. All I'm asking you to do is take a look.

No hitches." He pointed at the couch. "Have a seat right there, Mrs. Copeland."

She did.

Surprised, he knelt down and laid the Warner box flat. He removed the lid and propped it up so that the brand name, boldly embossed in red, faced the couch. He quickly laid out the Warner's key parts and accessories, various colored plastic nozzles and hoses, in a neat little row to his side. Then he took the snub-nosed power plant out of the box, slowly removed the plastic bag from it, and set it on the carpet. With its sleek curves and molded aluminum, it'd always reminded him of the back half of a forties Ford sedan.

"The Warner," he said, slapping his palms against his thighs.

Sandy pursed her brow as she took a long drag on her cigarette.

"Oh, for Christ's sake," she said, suddenly bursting out with a throaty laugh. She set her cigarette in the ashtray. "My mother had one of those." She leaped out of her seat, startling him, and knelt down on the floor. She picked up the power plant, ran her fingers all over it. "Put the product in the customer's hands," Dawn always said. If only it'd been that easy every time.

"I can't believe it," she said, running the power plant back and forth on the carpet. "My mother used to let us kids play with this thing, like a toy. I haven't seen one in thirty years. I didn't know they still made them."

"These things can really take a beating."

"You can say that again." She picked the power plant up in her hands and spun one of the plastic wheels. She glanced quickly up at Paul, then back to the power plant. "My brother, Jimmy, he used to kick this thing around the floor like it was a soccer ball. He'd pretend it was a tank and he'd throw baseballs at it, like a bazooka shell or something. He was a crazy kid. Always pounding on things." She shook her head. "You know what he said to my husband on our wedding day? 'Treat her right or I'll kick your ass.' Dean almost wet his pants."

They both laughed. Sandy leaned forward, hands on her knees, and bowed her head, shoulders shaking with gaiety. Paul couldn't believe his luck; he thought he might have something going. Maybe Dawn was right, after all. Then Sandy's shoulders quit moving for a second and she brought a fist up to her mouth. She started coughing—great, huge, raspy coughs, about six of them. She stopped and patted her chest a couple times. She was still bent forward. Paul asked her if she was okay, and she held up her index finger and nodded. A moment later she lifted her face to him and he saw that her eyes were wet. She raised her eyebrows and tilted her head a little to her left side and he thought for a second she was going to cry. That, or keel over. It was an awkward moment. He tried to think of something to say to steer them back.

"Where's he now?"

After a long pause, she said, "Florida."

"Really? That's a great golf state. What's your brother do there?"

"Jimmy?"

"Yeah."

"Jimmy lives in Las Vegas. He runs security at a hotel."

"Oh." He picked up a red plastic nozzle, turned it over once in his hand, then set it back down.

Sandy coughed once more, then said, "I've got to quit smoking." She smiled as she picked up the power plant and set it down before him. "This thing is a lot lighter than I remember."

"It's a new model."

The smile dropped from her face. "Yeah, there's always a new model." She climbed back up onto the couch, then took her glass from its coaster and took a long swallow. She settled back into the cushions. Her gaze moved to the painting above the fireplace. "Forget Scotland, Paul. Forget golf. Go to Las Vegas. You're young. Blackjack and twenty-four-hour buffets. And the women. You know what I'm saying?" She looked at him and raised her eyebrows.

His eyes dropped to the Warner and all the parts laid out in absurd little rows, color coded for function. He still had to pee.

"Do you mind if I smoke a cigarette?"

"Be my guest, sweetheart."

He took his Camels from his shirt pocket and lit one. Then he had a drink of water. He started talking about the Warner in no particular order, forgetting the script, not worrying about what Dawn would say if she knew what he was doing. He talked about the adjustable head lamp, the two-speed motor, the dual fan system. He unwrapped the thirty-two-foot power cord, which, he pointed out, could conceivably allow you to clean your house using only two or three outlets.

Sandy sat quietly on the couch, chain-smoking Virginia Slims. But she was listening.

"The Warner power plant moves 152 cubic feet of air per minute," he said. "Again, with the dual fan system, you can suck it up or pump it out, depending on the configuration." He lit another Camel. "Now, I know your mother had one of our older models. And as great a machine as that Warner was, I've got to tell you they've made milestones since. For example, did you know that your new Warner can function as an air compressor?"

"Ho ho. Not my Warner. I can tell you right now, sugar, I'm not in the market."

"Gotcha. But let me just show you something. You'll love this. Did you know that you can pump up your car tires with this thing? Would you like that?"

"If I had a car, maybe."

"Fair enough. How about a paint sprayer, or a furniture cleaner? Do you go to the lakes? I bet you go over to Lake Harriet all the time. This little number can pump up your air mattress."

"Don't go to the beach."

"Really? That's fine, Mrs. Copeland. The water's filthy there, anyhow. I never go either. Who needs it? That's the beauty of the Warner system. If you don't need an air compressor, no problem. Your new Warner does so many other things, you'll never even miss it."

"I told you I'm not in the market," she snapped. It felt like being hit with an ice-cold bucket of water.

"I'll tell you something, Paul. Mr. Salesman. You should've been here a month ago, okay? My husband just loves this kind of crap. He'd have been your sale." She stood from the couch and picked up her cigarette pack. "This was amusing for a while, but I'm bored now. I've got . . . I've got things to do, you know? I'm going downtown in a little while. Okay, so I don't have a car. You want to know what I need? I need a car. I have to take the bus downtown, do you understand?"

She closed her eyes, brought her cigarette to her lips, and took a long drag.

"Mrs. Copeland, I—"

"—You know what it's like to look for a job, don't you, Paul? The buses run every half hour and you have to have exact change. It pays to have a car. You're right about that."

He nodded once, slowly. He took a long, final drag off his cigarette, then leaned over and dropped the butt, still burning, into the ashtray. They looked at each other for a long moment. Sandy narrowed her eyes at him and crinkled up her nose a little, as if she were suddenly asking herself what in the world he was doing there in her living room with all that crap spread out on the floor.

"I want to show you something," Paul said.

He quickly attached the filter to the exhaust port, opened it, and inserted a paper dirt pad. After snapping the wide-mouth suction head onto the front of the power plant, he attached the long, D-shaped handle to the top of the machine, converting the Warner into a hand-held portable. He picked up the Warner and a handful of paper dirt pads and stepped into the dining area.

"Which way to the bedroom?"

"What?"

"Is it through here?" He pointed down the hallway, then walked toward the front door. He stopped at the base of the stairs and turned. When Sandy appeared at the other end of the hallway he knew he still had a shot.

At the top of the stairs he turned right, into what looked to be the master bedroom. The shades were all pulled down. The air was warm and stale, faintly musty. A dim yellow light hung in the room. Sheets were strewn in a rumpled lump across the queen-sized bed. Paul looked for an outlet and found one behind a chair. He tossed the power cord to the floor like a coil of rope.

Sandy leaned against the door frame, her hands behind her back.

"You'd be surprised at what can accumulate in a mattress, Mrs. Copeland."

He clicked the Warner on, then moved the sheets to the foot of the bed. He dragged the hand-held mattress cleaner across the bed, pulling three strips before turning off the motor. He opened the filter and extracted the paper pad. A layer of gray-brown dust and silt lay on it, fine, light, and powdery. He walked over to Sandy and held it before her.

"Do you know what this is?"

She shook her head.

"Putrifatic body ash," he said, slowly. "It's not only your household dust and dirt, but the dead skin, the dried body fluids that we rub off in our sleep. It's what we leave of ourselves, what we leave behind. Over a period of years, even months, our mattresses, pillows, couches collect an enormous quantity of this stuff."

She stared at the pad in his hand, gently chewing her lower lip.

"It's a health thing. Germs. Viruses. The residue of who we are."

Sandy's eyes flashed up at him. Her chin quivered. She backed away from the door frame, bumping the door gently against the wall as she turned and walked downstairs.

Paul stood there for a moment with the pad in his hand, then walked over to the dresser and dropped it in a small plastic wastebasket. On the dresser were several picture frames. Black-and-whites of people in old-fashioned clothing. A color picture of two young boys standing barefoot on a dock, alongside a small lake. In the sky behind them, an arching rainbow. Sandy and a tall, trim man with dark hair greased back tightly against his scalp, arm-in-arm in front of the house he was now in. Sandy and the same man kissing in the middle of a dance floor, under piñatas and soft lights.

Paul loosened the knot of his tie and unfastened the top button of his shirt. He walked over to a window and pulled the shade back with his finger. His cream-colored Toyota sat alone in the avenue, baking in the sun. Spots of rust dotted the car's body like bullet holes. Or sores.

The beer can opened with a hiss. He lit another cigarette and leaned against the kitchen counter, flitting ashes into the sink. It'd felt so good to finally pee. He'd washed his hands and face in the sink and come to hang out in the kitchen for a couple of minutes before he shampooed Sandy's carpet. He wasn't in a rush anymore.

Several minutes later, she reappeared, wiping her eyes with a tissue. Her face looked red and puffy.

Paul held up the beer can. "You said anything in the fridge, right?"

"I think maybe you better leave now."

"I haven't done your shampoo yet."

"You don't have any idea . . ." Her voice trailed off weakly.

"Let's get started."

He took the small plastic shampoo attachment into the kitchen and filled it with hot tap water. He opened another beer and returned to the living room. Sandy sat cross-legged on the couch, watching him, but he was done talking. He picked up the briefcase and the cardboard box and put them on the couch next to her. After assembling the Warner into an upright and attaching the shampooer to the power plant, he began to lay down strip after strip of white foam.

After five minutes he felt the sweat trickling down his back. Sandy was sorting through the cardboard box, picking up attachment tubes and brushes. She held the spray gun in her hand, pulling the trigger. She rubbed the bristles of the Qwik Brush. Her mouth was moving, but the loud whir and hum of the shampooer blotted out the sound of her voice. From time to time she raised a tissue to her eyes. When he was on the last go of laying down the foam, she got up and left the room, the Qwik Brush and spray gun still in her hands.

Paul turned off the Warner. Millions of tiny bubbles were popping and bursting, filling the room with a steady, soft, relaxing sound. He wondered where Sandy had gone. He had to let the bubbles soak for at least fifteen minutes. He took his beer from the mantle of the fireplace, and that's when he saw the golf club sticking out of the umbrella stand next to the patio door. He picked up the club. It was an ancient iron, with a worn, slightly tarnished head and a blonde, wooden shaft. He read the embossment on the back of the clubhead.

> Mashie Niblick
> Warranted—Hand Forged
> Bob Croll Special
> Perth, Scotland

"Mashie niblick," Paul said. The sound of it made him smile. "Mashie niblick."

The varnish on the wood was brittle and cracking. It needed to be resealed. The red leather grip needed work, too. It was dry and slightly loose, with a wear spot near the top of the grip, right where you press the base of your left thumb into the leather. The club was probably worth a lot of money. Hand-crafted, for sure. The kind of club you would've used a hundred years ago at St. Andrew's.

He opened the screen door and stepped into the back yard. He took a couple of loose practice swings. The club was much too short for him, but he enjoyed holding it. He liked the feel, the heft of the clubhead as it swung around; it was much heavier than his Pings. When was this mashie niblick last used? It might've been sitting in that umbrella stand for twenty, thirty years. He lined up a small pine cone and swung, the clubhead cutting through the long grass with a swish. The pine cone flew, wobbly, in a short arc across the yard and hit the wooden fence with a soft *tock*. He took a sip of beer. The lawn was covered with pine cones, each of them begging to be knocked against the wooden fence.

When he returned to the living room he put the club back in the umbrella stand. The house was very quiet. The foam had soaked into the carpet and left a flaky white residue. He disconnected the shampooer and attached the Karpet Perk fluffer-buffer. He began to work over the carpet, sucking up the flakes, working slowly.

When he was half done, Sandy reappeared. She said nothing—didn't even look at him—but picked up a handful of Warner attachments from the box on the couch and left the room again. Her eyes looked glassy and she seemed a little out of it, like she'd forgotten he was there. Paul kept working. A few minutes later she returned and left with another armload.

She appeared one more time before he was done. She took his briefcase and the assortment of vacuum cleaner bags he'd laid next to it. She looked at him shortly, her face puffy and loose, and then was gone again.

Paul finished the last pass in the living room and turned off the engine. All she'd left were the cardboard box and the little plastic wrapping bags and foam inserts. He disconnected the power cord, wrapped it up and tossed it into the box. He quickly broke down the Warner and laid it all in the box on top of the cord. Then he moved the coffee table back into place. He looked around the room. The carpet actually did look better— the color was a little brighter and the nap was fluffed up—though the wear spots were still visible. He listened for Sandy but heard nothing.

He used the bathroom just off the hallway between the kitchen and the front door, then walked back to the kitchen. He took another beer out and opened it. He thought about where he would go when he left Mrs. Copeland's house. He sure as hell wasn't going back to the office. Too many questions. Dawn would want to know where his demo unit had gone. Had it been stolen? Had he quit? Somebody had to pay.

"Mrs. Copeland," he said once, loudly. "Sandy."

He walked back into the living room. The remains of the Warner sat where he'd left them. He sipped the beer. He looked again at the painting of St. Andrew's above the fireplace. A lawn mower came to life in the yard next door, the engine coughing and sputtering before settling into a high, steady hum.

He took the mashie niblick from the umbrella stand. He imagined himself on the eighteenth fairway at St. Andrew's, lined up, feet spread to shoulder's width, ball back in his stance, neck down, shoulders flat. He's one stroke behind in the Scottish Open. He brings the club back slowly. The blade of the iron meets the ball with a soft, metallic click. The clubhead swings up and over his left shoulder. The ball travels in a silent, graceful arc, a solitary white dot against the brilliant blue sky.

The shot goes in. He wins with an eagle. The crowd roars.

Mashie niblick.

He thought about that club, murmuring the name like a mantra, as he walked out of the house and crossed the front lawn, heading for his Toyota. He would re-wrap the grip himself. Tarnish remover would brighten and polish the clubhead. With a little work the old club would be looking almost new, a real prize, something to hold onto.

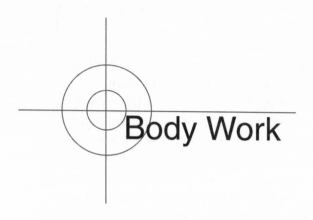

Body Work

I watched Barry drive the first car of the day, a green Chevy Impala, up to the garage, then get out and start looking it over, sizing it up. He walked across the small car lot quickly, his trousers a little too tight, his tie a little too wide. A little too much mousse in the hair, slicked back flat against his head.

I sat in the air-conditioned break room sipping coffee from a foam cup. Barry opened the door and closed it quietly behind him. He did that often, sneaking around the garage, office, and car lot, watching you.

"Got a job," he said, lifting his chin. "We need to paint that Chevy by noon."

"It won't be dry by noon."

"You think I don't know that?" He set the work order on the table in front of me with a thwack. "Just do the quickie." He clapped his hands. "Bing bang boom."

The work order was barely filled out, like a lot of the sheets he'd been giving me lately. A name but no address, no phone number. Terms of payment: cash on delivery. I'd let it go for three weeks.

"Seems you been getting kind of lazy filling these out."

He laughed once. "Lazy?"

"Well, let's see. A four-hour COD repaint. No proper work order. Either you're lazy, or we're painting a hot car."

He folded his arms across his chest. "The mind of a criminal at work."

I pushed the work order toward the center of the table with the tip of my middle finger. "You could get me in a lot of hot water, Barry."

"You're pretty good at doing that yourself, it seems."

I tilted my chair back on its two rear legs so my shoulder blades and neck rested against the cool plaster of the wall behind me.

"I'm just looking out for number one."

Barry took the gold pen from his shirt pocket. He drew it slowly across his top lip, like he was smelling a cigar. "Of course. You've got what, a month left on your probation?"

"Six weeks. I'm clear on September first. And I'm not screwing it up."

He put the pen back in his pocket, the same pen he handed to customers when they leaned across his desk to sign the papers for a used car. "Relax, James. Everyone here is simply doing their job. Your job is to paint cars. My job is to bring you that business. It's really very simple." He picked a bit of lint from his shirt cuff, pinching it between finger and thumb. "From now on, I'll fill out the work orders in detail, if that will appease your conscience."

I drummed my fingertips on the table and smiled.

He walked over to the coffee machine and picked up a

foam cup with "Coffee 25¢" written on the side. "Have you been putting in for coffee, James?" He set the cup back down and looked over at me, smiling again. "Free refills, but you have to pay for the first one." Then he walked out of the room, his loafers tapping on the vinyl-covered floor of the hallway.

I got up from the table and refilled my coffee cup, though I didn't need any more. The phone rang in Barry's office. His voice echoed in the small hallway. "Barry's Auto Emporium! How can I help you!"

I thought then of calling Evelyn. Maybe I'd call her at lunch, when I walked home to eat. I didn't really want to talk to the woman. She was my girlfriend's mother, that was all. But she treated me like a son-in-law, like I owed her something, even though Shelly and I had never come anywhere close to marriage. Evelyn was persistent, though. She'd left two messages on my machine the day before, asking me to call her. She'd called again that morning, right in the middle of breakfast, though I didn't answer it. I let the machine get it. "James, please give me a call." All polite and friendly. And this from a woman who once claimed in a court of law that she never want-ed her daughter to see or speak to me ever again.

If you listened to Evelyn—and that's all you did when you talked to her, believe me—it was my fault Shelly was drinking again. It was my fault she made those sud-den getaways. One time she'd gone up to Dallas, to see an old biker friend. Another time she'd ended up in San Antonio at a Motel 6. And, of course, she ran home a few times. God only knew where she'd run to this time, though to be honest I wasn't worrying much. Everyone has limits, and I'd about reached mine.

I left the office and walked across the car lot slowly, the cup of coffee hot in my hand. Out in the garage, Curl, the body repair guy, leaned against his work station, thumbing through an issue of *Hustler.* He was half singing along to "Don't Fear the Reaper" on KLOL, totally ruining a good song.

"Saw you in there talking to Fairy," he said. "Did he ask you to suck his dick?"

I set the coffee down on my small work station. "You wish." I pulled out my key ring and tossed it down on my desk. "It's business before pleasure for the ol' Bare. He's gone and got me another hot car to paint."

Curl laughed and scratched the fat that hung over the top of his work pants. He walked around in the same baggy black pants every day, his blue work shirt untucked, even though Barry had asked him twenty times if once to tuck it in and to wear a belt.

"At least he's getting you some work. The only bodies I seen in here for the last two days is these." He held up a centerfold for me.

"Yeah." I unlocked my storage cabinet and started getting the sander ready.

"Oh, sweet Jesus, look at those titties. Can't you see me going to work on top of that bitch?"

"You'd smother her."

"Damn straight. Total domination." He slapped his belly and tilted his head back and laughed. The sleeve of his work shirt was stained with something. Dried oatmeal, it looked like.

"Go get that Impala and drive it in here," I said.

"Yeah, yeah. Don't worry. Ain't nobody pissing in your Cheerios, James."

Curl knew that when I was working I didn't like to talk, so after he drove the Impala into the garage he took his magazine and disappeared somewhere. I worked quickly with the sander for a while, just hitting the big rust spots, the ones that anyone who knew anything about painting a car would look for. There were other spots too, of course, that needed more sanding, little places where the rust was just beginning to form. These spots needed closer attention, a finer grain of sandpaper. Everything needed to be scraped down to bare metal if the paint was going to do the car any good. You want the new coat to seal the car just like the original factory job did. It preserves and protects the body. And I liked that feeling of looking at a ten-year-old car that I'd just repainted. It's glossy-looking. Absolutely clean. But it's not just the looks that please. It's that feeling, knowing that the body is sealed, that I've done a good job, a thorough job, that the problems have been taken care of. That kind of work took time.

The first time I went cold turkey, I had to. And, maybe, when you don't have a choice, when you're locked up, it's easier. Not easy, just easier. I thought about drinking all the time. I lay on my bunk and thought over and over about the buzz you catch after two, three beers. I thought I was going crazy, surrounded by orange bars, brown walls, the smell of BO and piss. You can't hardly sleep for all the snoring and farting from the other guys in the cell. I thought what I needed was a drink, so I thought about drinking. You have to have something to keep you going.

Mel showed up on the fourth day. I don't even remember his last name, now. He was quiet and kept to himself, like a lot of guys do. He didn't want to play cards or dice or swap stories about the craziest shit he'd ever done. He was a short, skinny guy with a thick beard and long hair. Really pale skin. He had the bunk below mine, and one night, at dinnertime, we got to talking, like you do in a jail cell when there's nothing much else to do. Mel was a thief. He'd stolen a few TVs and sold them to some second-hand shops. It wasn't his first time getting locked up. He'd stolen cars, stereos, furniture. He said he figured it was his nature.

"Every time I get out of jail, I swear to God I ain't going to steal again. I stay clean a week or two, maybe a month. But comes a day you're just studying something. Thinking how you could steal that, sell it real fast. It's like that. You're doing it again 'fore you even realize you're doing it again."

"I know about that," I said.

"'Course you do, brother." He stroked his beard a couple of times. He was watching the card game in the corner, his gaze as steady and sharp as a cat's. "One time you stop yourself, so then you think you got it under control. But another time comes along and 'fore you know it, you've grabbed something. Then it's one-two-three. Sooner or later, every thief gets caught."

He turned to me on the bed, the mattress springs creaking as he shifted his weight. "I reckon I done what I knowed I'd do," he said. He lifted his bushy eyebrows. "I ain't an honest man. I'm a crook, and God knows it. Ain't no sense arguing it. If they let me out of here, I'll just go back to my crooked ways. So I ask Jesus to forgive me."

"Oh," I said. I saw it coming, then.

"The book of Daniel says, 'To the Lord belong mercy

and forgiveness.' And in Acts it's written, 'Every one who believes in Him receives forgiveness of sins through His name.'" He rolled up his shirt sleeve to show me his tattoo of Jesus on the cross. "Have you accepted your Savior into your heart, James? He bled for you. Have you bled for him?"

I was sorry I'd started talking to Mel after that, because he wouldn't shut up. Finally one of the other guys got sick of hearing the Jesus rap and threatened to pound Mel if he didn't knock it off.

I turned down the card game after dinner that night. I was thinking. Three DUIs and a previous assault conviction. It wasn't much. I was looking at a few weeks in jail. Less, if my lawyer came through. I'd get out eventually. Then what?

When I was a kid growing up in Conroe, my old man was gone a lot, out working rigs in the Gulf. Fifteen days on, fifteen days off. But when he was home he kept everyone in line. My mom, too. The littlest thing could set him off, and then look out. When you screwed up, he went nuts. He'd chase you around the house, the veins in his neck standing out like steel cords, his eyes wide with rage. He'd grab you and whip you with his belt, spittle flying in your face as he snarled, "Is your head screwed on, boy?"

It was his voice I heard in the dark that night—that angry, raspy voice. The slight slurring of his speech. I even smelled the whiskey on his breath. I lay in my bunk in that jail cell for a real long time, staring at the pock-marked cement ceiling. I'd bottomed out, I could admit that. Maybe my head wasn't screwed on. Maybe it never had been. But there's things you can do. You can say to yourself, I'm going to start over. Correct the mistakes. All of that. And it sounds good and real, talking like that. You believe it. You think you're strong enough.

I finished the Impala just before noon. I dropped the work order in the out-box, then checked the in-box for new orders. Sure enough, there were two sitting there. A crushed fender for Curl to pull out and a Toyota Tercel that needed a "custom" repaint. Curl was nowhere to be found, but that didn't surprise me. Odds were he was sucking on a Blizzard across the street at the DQ, or locked in the men's room. I was glad there'd be some decent work for me to do after lunch. It gave me something to look forward to.

As I clocked out, Barry called me into his office. He leaned against the edge of his desk, feet crossed at the ankles.

"See your work orders?"

"Yeah. Thanks."

"No problem. Effective communication between employer and employee and all that, right?"

I nodded.

"Say, what are you doing this weekend?"

I shrugged my shoulders. It wasn't a question I was in the mood to consider.

"You ought to jump with me. I think you'd love it, James. Really. Nothing clears out the system like a good leap from ten thousand feet. You feel . . ." He pointed at the photo on the wall of him flying through the air over Big Bend, the brown-and-red desert stretched flat as a tablecloth ten thousand feet below him. His legs and arms are spread straight out and a little upwards with the force of the wind. He's wearing a blue helmet and dark sunglasses and the biggest shit-eating grin you ever saw. Looking at that photo, you'd never guess in a million years how that man made a living.

"*That's* how you feel. Over five hundred jumps, and nothing worse than—"

"—I know, I know. A broken wrist."

He laughed. "Right."

"Not this weekend," I said. "I've got some repairs to do in the apartment before the lease is up."

"You're moving?"

I shrugged my shoulders. "Just seems like it's time to fix a couple things."

"*Comprendo.* But you let me know when you're ready to jump. I have the feeling you'll understand it."

I nodded just as the phone rang. Barry held up a finger as he reached for the receiver, but I turned and walked out of the office. He was always trying to sell you something.

People break promises all the time. You can't live a real life and not break promises. The trick is knowing which ones you can break and which ones you can't. I'm not talking about the law, though it could be that, for some people. I'm talking about those feelings you have in your heart. I'm talking about the things you just know you can't do because to do them would mean destroying yourself, who you are, what you want to be.

Shelly's drinking didn't upset me, at first. That's not how I took it. I took it like an invitation, like she was silently asking me to join her, to go back to the way we were when we'd first met. I even started thinking she was leaving clues. I found a book of matches from the

Idle Hour bar on the kitchen counter one day, a place we'd done a lot of drinking in at one time. Or I found an empty bottle of tonic water in the back seat of her car. There were other signs. Bottle caps in coat pockets. They're there if you're looking for them.

For a long time—several months—I'd tolerated her drinking, which only made my guts twist because I'd sworn never to do that again. How can you tolerate a drinker when it takes all you have just to stay sober every day, when you think about drinking all the time, when you feel possessed by something rather than in possession of it?

Things came to a head one day in June. We didn't have any work. I was really shagged and Barry was gone somewhere, so I sent Curl home, clocked out, and locked up the shop a couple hours early.

I smelled dope on the landing before I even had my hand on the doorknob. I threw the apartment door open, letting it slam back against the wall. A guy and a girl sat together on my couch. They had KLOL on and some drinks out on the coffee table. One of them turned his head to look at me. His face was bleary-eyed and slack. It was a guy named Tommy, a pothead who'd lived in Humble a couple of years ago and had dealt for a little while, until he got picked up.

"James," he said, laughing. "God damn, man. I thought you was a cop, busting in here like that."

"What's going on?" said the girl on the couch. She leaned forward and stared at the coffee table. "Which fucking drink is mine, now? Was I drinking beer?"

I crossed the living room, turned off the radio, and said, "Where's Shelly?"

Shelly came out of the bathroom wearing cut-off jeans and a tight yellow tank top. Her hair was pulled back in a ponytail and she said, "You guys, you guys." She was laughing about something, but then she saw me and stopped. The smile dropped clean off her face. She put a hand up on the wall to steady herself and said, "James," like she'd just found out her car tire was flat. "We were just leaving. I stopped by to pick up the, uh . . ."

"James, excellent," said Tommy, sitting forward on the couch. "Good to see you, man."

I turned around and took a step toward him. "Stand up," I said. "Stand up so I can knock you flat on your ass."

"Buzz kill," mumbled the girl on the couch.

Tommy brushed his long, straight hair back behind an ear. "Okay."

"James, don't," said Shelly. She fiddled with the half dozen silver bracelets around her wrist.

"If you're leaving, get the fuck out."

"You're pissed."

"Pissed? You're fixing to see pissed."

"I'm out of here," said the girl. She stood and collected the bottle of vodka and a beer from the table. She gave me a frown as she started for the door. "I know your kind."

Shelly scrunched up her eyes. "Are you threatening me?"

The girl stopped in the doorway. "Shelly, come on. Get out of his way now, huh?"

Shelly put her hands on her hips. "No, I want to know. Are you threatening me, James? 'Cause I'll call the fucking cops. You want that? You want to go back to jail?"

"*Hasta la vista*, baby," said Tommy, climbing over the back of the couch and walking quickly around the far side of the living room. He ran out the door and down the stairwell.

"Shelly, come on," said the girl.

"He won't touch me," Shelly said.

I took a step back, toward the empty couch. My boot heel touched the leg of the coffee table. Shelly and I looked at each other for a long moment. Her jaw was set tight. Brown eyes; long, kinky golden hair; thin arms; the scar on her left knee from a car accident when she was sixteen: I had known and loved every inch of that body. But at that moment . . . I don't even have the words for it. It's beyond my understanding.

I reached down to the table, picked up a full beer bottle and threw it against the wall, just left of the door. It knocked a hole about the size of a coffee mug in the plaster, then fell to the carpet, unbroken.

She ran then, leaving the door open onto the empty hallway. Her footsteps echoed in the stairwell. I threw myself onto the couch. I did nothing for a long time. Didn't even close the apartment door. If I put together the half-empty glasses of vodka and the beers they'd left, I probably had a good six drinks sitting there. Enough to catch a buzz. I picked up an unopened beer. Beads of condensation dripped over my fingers like sweat.

I held that bottle for a long minute, then I set it back on the table and lit a cigarette and smoked it.

After a little while everything started to come down to earth. It's good when you can do that: just stop the building anger, the crazy feelings. I wish I could do that more often. I smoked another cigarette and started to clean up the apartment. I had to toss all those bottles before I started thinking about drinking them again. Walking around the living room with the garbage can, I felt the familiar tightness in my shoulders—the feeling that someone was pressing his thumbs into the base of my skull with all his strength. In another twenty minutes I'd have a monster headache. I scraped the table clean: bottles, cups, even the ashtray with the roaches. I walked over by the front door and picked up the bottle I'd thrown. Little bits of plaster clung to the cap. If I'd opened it right then, it would have exploded.

I tossed the bottle in the trash can.

I left the building and went outside. It was crazy, but at that particular moment, walking barefoot across the warm asphalt of the parking lot with the heavy garbage can in my hands, violence felt inevitable. All those anger management workshops, all the things they tell you to do like count to ten, or repeat a "mantra," or think of something pleasant—it all seemed like a bunch of crap.

You try to be patient. You try to put up with all the shit in your life, but you know what? Sometimes that's the whole problem. An alcoholic can't live with a problem drinker. Period. A girl with a thing for tough guys—a girl who hasn't got the guts to stay gone when she runs—she shouldn't be with a guy like me. Not if she can't stick to her promises.

I hoisted the garbage can up and tilted it into the dumpster. The bottles clanked and glass tinkled as some of them broke. The dumpster smelled of warm, moist garbage. A rotting smell. There were flies out there, and a scrawny little cat making noise. It was no place to linger.

I spent my lunch break in my apartment, watching

the mid-day news and eating a sandwich. As I washed up in the bathroom, I decided to call Evelyn after all. Knowing her, she'd start calling me in the middle of the night pretty soon, if she thought it was important enough. And everything Evelyn sets her mind to is important, if you know what I mean. I stretched out on the couch with the cordless phone and dialed her number. Her voice appeared on the line immediately, gruff and raspy as always.

"Yeah." I heard a TV show blaring in the background. One of her soaps.

"It didn't even ring," I said.

"It rang here once, darling." She muted the TV. "I keep the phone right next to me. Never know who'll be calling."

I waited a moment, then said, "So, you called here a couple times."

"Yeah, I did. Aren't you ever home? Where were you at seven-thirty this morning?"

"In the shower. What'd you want?"

"It's about Shelly."

I waited. I mean, she'd called me first. Plus, you had to put up with so much bullshit every time you talked to Evelyn, it's a wonder you ever got around to actually saying anything. The less words, the better.

"I'm worried about her this time, James. You know who she's with?"

"No, and I don't care."

"She's in Pasadena with a guy named Tommy. She says you know him."

"Yeah, I know him."

"She's in trouble, James. Real trouble. Next to him, you're a rose, do you understand? This one isn't taking care of her at all."

"She's a big girl now. She ought to be looking after herself."

"Do you know he had the nerve to call and ask me to send Shelly money? He said she was broke and really down on her luck and could use a little help. I ought to send her some money right away. He wanted to know why I was holding out on my daughter. He wanted to know what kind of mother I was. I don't think she knew he made that call. She would never have let him say those things to me."

I held my tongue for a moment, then said, "So why call me?"

"She hasn't called in over a week, James. I cussed that man out and told him to put Shelly on the phone but then he called me a name I will not repeat and hung up on me. After that, no calls for five days. You're the first. It's not like her not to call me when she's running around like this. I think it's that man she's taken up with. He's no good."

"I get you."

I heard the *flick-flick-flick* of her lighter, and then, a moment later, the first exhale after a freshly lit cigarette. "I never thought I'd say this about you, but you're a better man than he is, James. You'd never say the things he said to me. Imagine, his going behind her back to call me and ask for money. And then to insult me? How do you suppose he got my number?"

She gave it to him, we both knew that. But I said, "I suppose he watched her dial it."

"Now, listen, I don't want you going out there and busting any heads open."

I cleared my throat. "If you're asking me to rescue her, forget it."

"Hang on a sec." I heard her toss the phone down and the sound of coughing from another part of the trailer. She hacked something up, into the kitchen sink, I imagined. Then she picked up the phone and said, "You remember my birthday?"

"What?"

"Two years ago. She hadn't told me y'all was coming, and believe me, it was a surprise."

I grunted. What I remembered about that day was how damn hot Evelyn's trailer was. It was late April, but it was warm. She never ran the AC until May, she'd said, and wouldn't open the windows on account of the ragweed.

"She'd gotten a new haircut, short, and she wore a nice new blouse and a skirt, even. I remember thinking how she looked so healthy and happy. She spent an entire day with me. We sat on the couch and drank iced tea and talked."

"I remember. You made me eat three pieces of rum cake." Which gave me a stomachache and indigestion.

She laughed. "That's the day I keep in my mind, James. I don't understand what's happened before or since, but I keep that one day in my mind."

I remembered that day a little differently. I recalled a bit of quarreling out on the porch, and a request that I keep my nose out of what didn't concern me. But I let that pass.

"Evy, listen. I got to get back to work. I understand what you're asking, but Shelly and me, we just aren't on the same level anymore. We've been kind of lingering on, both thinking we might find a way to work it out, but it's no good. This thing ain't ending on a clear line, so I'm drawing one. So, it's been good talking to you, you know?"

She sniffled. "You think this is a joke. You think I'm a lonely old woman living in a trailer in the woods. You think I have nothing better to do than sit around feeling sorry for myself."

"God, no."

"I know you do." She blew her nose. Then she started laughing, which struck me as odd. "You know, you and me, James. We're exactly alike."

"How's that?"

"We're never going to know true happiness."

The sound of those words in her raggedy old mouth stopped me for a minute. "No," I said.

"You don't want to believe it, I know. But some people in this world are always making big plans. And it's funny. They don't ever seem to get anywhere." There was the sound of silverware clattering on plates, like she was serving lunch, or doing the dishes. "She told me about your last tantrum. She said you threw a beer bottle at her. She said you threatened to hit her again."

I looked across the room to the broken plaster near the door. "I threw a bottle at the wall."

"You threw that bottle at her! I'll never understand why my daughter ever went back to you. I didn't pay for that assault conviction just so she could go slinking back to your bed six weeks later. You owe her, James, and you know it."

I rubbed the bridge of my nose with my fingertips. I closed my eyes and took a couple of deep breaths. Nothing I would've said at that moment would've been very nice, so I disconnected and dropped the cordless to the floor.

After a few minutes I went into the kitchen to get something but forgot what it was and instead I sat down in a chair and smoked a cigarette. My shoulders were tensing up again, all of that. I felt like I needed to hit something.

Behind our apartment building, just beyond the parking lot and the smelly old dumpster, was a strip of burned-out grass thirty feet wide lined by a flimsy post-and-beam fence. The pine trees started just beyond the fence, right there, a stone's throw from our kitchen window. The trees were tall, eighty or ninety feet, and had scaly bark coated with thick, sticky sap. The branches didn't start until about halfway up, and stuck straight out from the trunk, then curved upwards just a little. Like Barry's arms when he jumped.

Shelly never liked the trees behind our apartment. They gave her the creeps. Anybody could walk out of there, she used to say, break into our apartment and steal something. Rape her. Whatever. She used to keep the mini-blinds down in the kitchen so she didn't have to look at them, which seemed crazy to me. I loved those trees. Day or night, there was a darkness there, thick and impenetrable. No amount of staring would lessen it.

When I finished my cigarette, I lit another. Work could wait. I needed to get my bearings. I needed to remind myself what was important: that it's possible to be happy in this life.

There's only one thing stronger than alcohol, and that's love. But there are different kinds of love, and they aren't all equal. They can't be.

I spent a good two hours wet-sanding the Tercel, since the original paint wasn't too bad. I covered up the windows and chrome with tape and plastic. I jacked the car up and removed the tires. When I have time to do it right, painting a car can be really relaxing. It's like meditation or something. Hours go by and you don't notice because everything feels full, complete. You're in control.

I was just getting ready to prime the car when Curl drove up in a cream-yellow Caddy with some serious damage, side-impact stuff. The windshield was cracked and a window had been busted out.

"Looks like you'll have your hands full, for a change," I said.

"I wish. Fairy says do this one now."

"What? Paint that? Paint over a bashed-in door?"

Curl shrugged his shoulders and plunged his hands into his pockets. "He just said do it. Any color. The cheapest color."

"Fuck him. I'm in the middle of this one. I won't get to it until tomorrow."

"He said do it now."

"Where's the work order?"

"He didn't give me none."

"Barry can shove it up his ass. You go back to the office and tell him no work order, no work. He'll know what I mean."

I turned away from Curl and switched on the air compressor. The hum drowned out the radio and the highway traffic. I pulled my goggles down over my eyes and began covering the Toyota in gray primer. Curl stuck around while he figured out what to do, rolling his head on his shoulders and mumbling to himself. Then he ambled out of the garage.

Twenty minutes later Barry stormed in, his thin frame stiff and erect. I stepped back from the Toyota and turned off the sprayer. The sound of the radio and Curl's tools clinking on the other side of the garage slowly filled my ears. I lifted my goggles.

Barry shot a finger over to the Cadillac. "Why aren't you painting that car?"

"Because I'm in the middle of this job," I said, pointing at the Toyota with my thumb. "Besides, there's no work order."

"I said do it. That's the only order you need."

I took off my work gloves, then turned and placed them on my work station. I closed my eyes and started counting to ten, slowly.

Barry walked around the Toyota, his shoes crunching on the rust scattered across the shop floor. He put his hand on my shoulder and gave it a firm squeeze. "I'm not asking you, James."

I opened my eyes. "Get your hand off me."

He removed his hand, then stepped to my side. He put an elbow up on the work station and looked at me for a moment. He took the gold pen out of his pocket and tapped my wrist with it gently, once.

"James."

I spun around, grabbed him by the shirt collar, and

pushed him back against the open door of my tool cabinet, which slammed shut with a loud crash. Nose to
nose, I said, "You're not listening to me. You don't fucking get it, do you?"

He raised a hand weakly to my chest. His eyes blinked
rapidly.

"Think about what you're doing," he stammered.
"You're asking for big trouble. This is assault. Battery.
You'll go to jail for assaulting me!"

I slowly loosened my grip. I'd been leaning my elbows
into his ribs, pressing him against the case with all my
weight. I let go of his shirt, stepped back, mumbled an
apology.

"God damn, James." It was Curl. He stood a few feet to
my right, his mouth wide open, arms limp at his side. His
cheeks were streaked with lines of grease, like war paint.

"What're you looking at?"

He whistled and shook his head. "God damn, James."

"Get back to work, you damn grease monkey."

His face broke into a wide, sinister smile, like he
thought he knew something then, the dumb tub of shit.
But he turned and walked back to the Duster.

Barry had stepped away from me, out of reach. We
looked at each other for a long moment. "Look," I said,
"I'm sorry. Sometimes I bust a nut. I fucking lose it. I've
just been kind of stressed out and—"

He cut me off with a curt wave of his hand, then
smoothed his shirt front and adjusted his tie. "There's
nothing to explain. I should know better than to hire . . .
temperamental individuals." He rubbed his neck with
his hand, as if he'd been whiplashed. "I would hate to

have to bring charges against you, James. And with an eyewitness to boot. Surely if you just returned to work and did what your employer asked of you a trifling outburst like this could be forgotten."

I stared at him for several seconds. His eyes were bright again, defiant, and part of me felt like decking him once and for all. A year in jail might be worth it.

"Go ahead. Call the cops. When they ask how it started, I'll be glad to tell them."

Barry's eyes flashed to the Caddy, then back to me. "I suppose you think you're clever."

"Just looking out for number one."

"So you've said." He ran a finger along the inside of his shirt collar. "So okay, no one calls the cops."

Curl was crouched on the far side of the Plymouth, smiling and nodding his head. He looked at me and lifted his eyebrows.

"What're you looking at, asshole?"

He sputtered out a laugh, and then started pounding on the fender again.

Barry folded his arms across his chest. He spoke softly. "I still need this Caddy painted by five o'clock, or else."

"Don't threaten me, Barry. I don't need that."

"No, no. Not trouble for you." He tapped his chest with a finger.

I sat down on a stool. I picked up a towel, wiped my hands, and tossed it into the corner. "So you've got problems. Welcome to the fucking club."

Barry turned to face me, with his back to Curl's half of the garage. "I know you don't want to do this, James. So

I'll make it worth your while." He took a roll of money out of his pocket, and, holding it close to his belly, peeled off a hundred-dollar bill and handed it to me. "Let's just say I really need this one painted."

I looked at that bill for way too long. It was one of the new ones, with the big portrait on it. I don't know what I was waiting for. It's not like I believe in omens. What I will say is this: as soon as I took it, I felt a line of dominoes begin to click and fall inside me. I still feel it to this day.

Barry smiled and let out a sigh. "Thank you, James. You have no idea—"

"—I'll paint your Caddy if you lend me a car this weekend."

He lifted his eyebrows. "What?"

"I'll have the Caddy done by five if you lend me a car. No questions asked."

He took a step back. "That's impossible."

"I doubt it."

He looked at his watch and then back at me. He lifted his chin. "You'd have the car back on the lot by seven o'clock Monday morning?"

"If it's not, I'll give you this C-note back." I folded the bill and slid it into my pants pocket.

He stepped close to me and whispered, "Don't you ever tell anyone what we're agreeing to, understand?"

"Back off, Barry. I've got a car to paint." I stood from the stool and hollered for Curl.

I waited until both Curl and Barry had left for the day, then locked up the garage. The Dodge, a rusty little four-door, was in the back row of the lot, hidden in a corner. I washed the "$500 Down!" off the windshield with a little warm water, then put the dealer plates in the back window. The car started on the third try. It smelled musty, like somebody had left a wet towel in there. No AC, of course, and 135,000 miles. I rolled down the windows and pulled out onto FM 1960. The gas gauge was on empty. Barry, that cheapskate, he drained every tank when he got a car. But I had a hundred bucks in my pocket. I'd fill her up, buy a cheeseburger, and head out to Pasadena. I knew a bar where I'd start looking. I didn't know if I'd find Shelly or not, or how all this would end. It didn't matter, really. A few early stars were out, and the sky was still pink to the west. In front of me was the familiar, endless stream of red taillights. I knew it was a beginning.

About the Author

Rob Davidson is Instructor of English at Purdue University in West Lafayette, Indiana.